The Bull Slayers

Inspector Faro, travelling incognito on the Queen's secret business, is sent to the Borders to clear the name of Bertie, Prince of Wales, who is involved in a scandal that could jeopardize his future as king.

Faro's reluctance to play royal spy proves justified when he steps from the streets of nineteenth-century Edinburgh into an alien land, an ancient bloodsoaked battlefield where England and Scotland clashed arms and the old ballads still cry out for vengeance. Here the powerful Elrigg family rule like feudal barons, owning everything and everyone, including the forces of law and order.

Travelling with Faro is the mysterious Imogen Crowe, whose business in Elrigg is obscure, but there is no one in whom the Inspector can confide, for the deceptive grandeur of a wild land hides sinister forces at work. The white cattle of the Borders roam dangerously free, and equally dangerous are the Elriggs, in their proud descent from fierce reivers with long memories for revenge.

But murder has been committed, and Faro is alone in his relentless pursuit of the truth, pitting his wits against an unseen enemy in a society where murders are dismissed as accidents. Scorning modern weapons, the Elriggs hunt their prey with bow and arrow and, unable to call upon the local police for assistance, Faro becomes a target for their deadly games.

By the same author

A Drink for the Bridge
The Black Duchess
Castle of Foxes
Colla's Children
The Clan
Estella
Enter Second Murderer
Blood Line
Deadly Beloved
Killing Cousins
A Quiet Death
To Kill a Queen
The Evil That Men Do
The Missing Duchess
Inspector Faro and the Edinburgh Mysteries (Omnibus edition)

non-fiction
The Robert Louis Stevenson Treasury
Stevenson in the South Seas
Bright Ring of Words

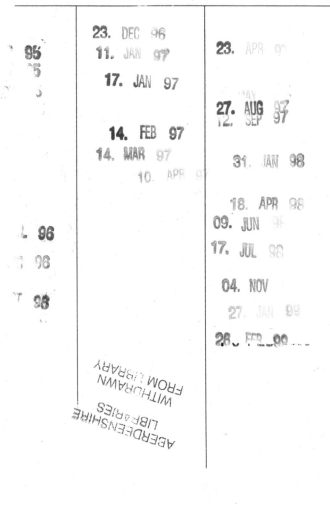

The Bull Slayers

An Inspector Faro Mystery

Alanna Knight

MACMILLAN

First published 1995 by Macmillan London

an imprint of Macmillan General Books
Cavaye Place London SW10 9PG
and Basingstoke

Associated companies throughout the world

ISBN 0 333 62960 4

9 8 7 6 5 4 3 2 1

A CIP catalogue record for this book is available from
the British Library

Phototypeset by Intype, London
Printed by Mackays of Chatham PLC, Chatham, Kent

MYS
909973

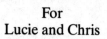

For
Lucie and Chris

Chapter 1

'It will be our secret . . .'

As Detective Inspector Jeremy Faro walked briskly away from the Palace of Holyroodhouse, the Queen's words echoed through his footsteps.

'It will be our secret, Inspector Faro.' And stretching out a small white hand, still girlish despite her increasing bulk, she had beamed on him.

There was no encouraging or polite smile from Faro as he returned the letter. He was reeling from the words he had just read. Momentarily speechless, watching her fold and replace in a drawer what might be damning evidence, enough to hang an ordinary man in a court of law, he gasped out: 'Your Majesty – would it not be, er, advisable perhaps to destroy that?'

The Queen was very small, and neither Faro nor anyone else was permitted to sit in the Royal Presence. It would never have occurred to her to be thus thoughtful, that a chair might be welcome to one of her loyal subjects who walked considerable distances each day.

Although Faro towered over her by more than a foot, she was not in the least intimidated since she froze statesmen twice as big as herself on any day of the week.

'We take it that you are not indicating that His Royal Highness is in any way involved in this unfortunate affair,' she said sternly.

Faro was doing exactly that, but thought better of it. He shook his head, in a valiant attempt to banish the ghastly realization taking shape as the Queen's glance changed to

1

one of icy displeasure calculated to demolish even a senior detective of the Edinburgh City Police. If looks could have killed . . .

The imperial hand moved in a gesture of airy dismissal. 'You have our permission to withdraw, sir.'

As Faro bowed himself out of her presence, followed by that ferocious glare, she added: 'His Royal Highness is quite innocent. Oh yes, entirely innocent, we expect you understand that.'

Faro didn't understand in the slightest, after the condemnation he had just read. Bewildered and with that sharp reprimand ringing in his ears as the footman closed the door on the Royal Presence, he marched smartly past equerries, attendants and various hangers-on hopeful of achieving an audience.

Moments later he emerged thankfully into the frivolous breeze of Holyrood Gardens.

'Sir . . . Follow me, if you please.'

A breathless footman waving frantically indicated that the Royal Command was still in operation. As Faro was wondering what further nonsense Her Majesty had in mind, he was led into the equally intimidating presence of her Prime Minister, with whom it must be confessed Inspector Faro had never been on the best of terms.

Ushered into Mr Gladstone's sanctuary, he noted that gentleman consulting his watch in the urgent manner of one who suspects that every waiting second is diminishing his not inconsiderable bank balance. And that those who wasted his time would find themselves in deep trouble.

At Faro's approach the gold watch was closed with a snap and returned to the Prime Minister's breast pocket.

'Further to your interview with Her Majesty, I must impress upon you the importance of your assignation. That on no account must you involve or invoke the Edinburgh Police. And that includes your Superintendent. Absolute confidentiality is vital. Do I make myself clear?'

'So Her Majesty has given me to understand. That is precisely why I am to go incognito.'

2

'A new role for you.' Gladstone's thin-lipped smile was mirthless. 'Her Majesty may have neglected, er, omitted to inform you of two paintings at Elrigg she is keen to possess?'

Without waiting for Faro's response, he continued: 'One is of His Royal Highness the Prince of Wales with a wild bull from the Elrigg cattle herd, shot on a previous visit. Her Majesty is very keen to have it for Balmoral. Painted by Landseer, of course. The other painting is of the state visit of King George the Fourth to Edinburgh. The Family is very sentimental about such connections and His Royal Highness has informed his mother how it reminds him of his late father. Hence her interest,' he added with a knife-like smirk.

While Faro was considering a tactful response and how anyone with reasonable eyesight could see any likeness between such dissimilar men, Mr Gladstone came rapidly to the point.

'Unfortunately His Royal Highness discovered on his recent visit that the two paintings had disappeared from the Castle. Stolen, he was told. No one knew quite how or when.'

He sighed heavily. 'We expect that you will do your best to recover these two items and acquire them for Her Majesty. This part of your, er, duty is, I need not tell you,' he added, heading Faro to the door, 'of a most secret nature.'

Secret, indeed. Her Majesty's childlike greed regarding possessions, especially paintings for her ever-growing col-lection, was as well known as her childlike delight in sec-rets. Regarding possessions, however, few were ever bought, most were acquired – demanded from their owners who, according to Her Majesty, had been 'pleased and honoured' to hand them over to her.

The Elriggs, however, had forestalled her. Even as the Prime Minister spoke, Faro had already put together one or two ideas of where they might be found. Knowing human nature, he did not envisage any problem in solving this particular mystery, the easiest part of his assignment.

Much more serious was the Prince's possible involvement in the mysterious death of his equerry, Sir Archie Elrigg. Faro, who had total recall where documents were concerned, found himself seeing again the letter Bertie had written to his mother, a damning but oddly boyish epistle, stressing the very unfortunate coincidence that on an earlier visit to Elrigg, a fellow guest, an actor, had also met with a fatal accident while they were out riding together.

'It was not *my* fault, Mama.' There was a whining note of schoolboy complaint as if such communications were regular and betrayed a desperate anxiety to get in his excuses before the headmaster's report had a chance to raise the parental wrath.

Presumably Her Majesty's anxiety was capable of innocent interpretation, as a fond mother's desire to protect her firstborn and to prove to herself that the future King of England had nothing at all to do with the extraordinary coincidence of two fatal accidents during his visits to Elrigg. Her particular concern was his equerry's unfortunate end, an almost desperate anxiety to prove to all who knew him the impossibility that Bertie could be guilty of the eighth deadly sin for the English gentleman: cowardice. Bertie had left an injured comrade to face the enemy, in this case a wild bull.

Such monstrous accusations had destroyed many a noble family. Less exalted men than princes had been forced by an unforgiving society to take the 'decent way out' while loading a conveniently inefficient shotgun.

Redemption was the name of that particular game. But in a royal house, there existed an even more sinister motive: the anxiety of a ruling monarch whose reprobate son's conduct failed to live up to the high moral standards implanted on the unwholesome Georgian society at her coronation. Such standards, admirable for the nation, were totally ignored by the heir to the throne as he lusted after yet another actress or society beauty.

Nor could his mother forgive or forget that his affair with actress Nellie Clifton while at Cambridge University had contributed to the premature death of her beloved Albert and her long and bitter widowhood.

In a poignant letter announcing his visit (and carelessly abandoned in Bertie's rooms at Madingley Hall), Prince Albert had written: 'You are the cause of the greatest pain I have ever felt in my life. You must not, you dare not be lost. The consequences for the country, for the world, would be too dreadful.'

But Bertie remained unrepentant, an unwilling student who stated publicly that he 'preferred men to books and women to either'.

After her husband's death, the Queen wrote that she never could or would look at their son without a shudder. Her hopes for his marriage in 1863 to Princess Alexandra of Denmark – 'one of those sweet creatures' (she wrote) 'who seem to come from the skies to help and bless poor mortals' – were doomed to disappointment as the bridegroom soon demonstrated an easy ability to accommodate a wife as well as a succession of mistresses.

Faro felt sympathetic; knowing a great deal more than would ever be made public about His Royal Highness's 'scrapes', he could understand Her Majesty's concern about the future of Britain.

'If he succeeds, he will spend his life in one whirl of amusements. There is a very strong feeling against the frivolity of society, everyone comments upon my simplicity.'

Simplicity was admirable, Faro thought, remembering her words, but cowardice never. For if coward Bertie was, leaving one man – his equerry – to be gored to death by a wild bull, how in heaven's name would he deal with the future of whole regiments of soldiers and the glory that was the ever expanding British Empire.

Faro sighed. As for understanding, he was certain of only one thing, that he was being asked, or rather commanded, to divert the course of justice if necessary on what might well turn out to be yet another royal scandal involving the future King.

It was a hopeless investigation with a trail long cold, Sir Archie dead and buried while the Queen had taken some time to decide whether or not she should take the Prime Minister's advice regarding her son's letter.

The situation was by no means unique. In the past, Royal persons had been revealed as suspiciously close to fatal accidents. The pages of history books were littered with prime examples. But such knowledge offered little consolation to the man whose unpleasant job was to throw a bucket of whitewash over the sordid business at Elrigg. Especially a man whose instinct for justice was equally as unyielding as his sovereign's moral code.

'There'll be a knighthood in it for you,' smirked Superintendent McIntosh, who had been eagerly awaiting the outcome of Faro's summons to the Palace of Holyroodhouse. In the unhappy position of following instructions in the form of a Royal command that his chief detective was to be granted leave of absence to undertake a personal and confidential mission for Her Majesty, he tried with difficulty to conceal his curiosity.

Regarding Faro narrowly, he signed the paper releasing him from duty. The Inspector had done it all before many times, of course, protecting Her Majesty and the Realm, but never with such secrecy. What were things coming to when a superintendent of highest character and spotless record could not be trusted with such confidential information?

'Thank you, sir,' said Faro. 'I'll be back as soon as I can.'

'Do that,' was all that McIntosh could say in the circumstances. 'Do you need anyone – McQuinn, perhaps? I could spare him.'

'That's very good of you, sir, but that would be complicated.'

'In what way? I mean, you will be in Edinburgh, of course?'

Faro shook his head. 'No, not even in Scotland.'

McIntosh's eyebrows disappeared into his hairline.

'I won't be far away though, just over the border, only a day's ride. And now, sir, if you'll excuse me.'

Nodding agreement, a very puzzled McIntosh went to the window and watched Faro leave the building and head across the High Street, as if such action might reveal some indication of his plans.

With a sigh he returned to his desk. Borders, eh. Then this could not be a police matter, hence his own exclusion from the details. Besides the English police had very different ideas of how the law should be administered and were, as far as he was concerned, a race apart.

No doubt time would reveal all.

Faro, however, hoped most fervently that it would not as he walked rapidly homewards through the crowded odorous High Street and emerged at last in the quiet villa quarters of Newington.

All around him Edinburgh blossomed, touched with the gentle splendour of Maytime. Arthur's Seat, proud and majestic, bloomed richly under the gold of broom while roadside hedgerows and gardens beguiled him with the scent of hawthorn blossom, of meadowsweet and delicate wild irises marching in sedate regiments shaded by mighty trees.

He breathed deeply. The warm breeze and gentle sunlight carried sweet odours of new grass and distant peat fires.

Approaching the tree-lined avenue leading to Sheridan Place with its handsome Georgian houses, he observed his housekeeper, Mrs Brook, industriously polishing the brass plate outside the home he shared with his stepson: DR VINCENT B. LAURIE, FAMILY PHYSICIAN, to which a new name, DR STEPHEN BALFOUR, had been added recently, a partner to accommodate the growing practice in this ever expanding suburb of prosperous merchants.

Mrs Brook looked up at his approach. 'This is a grand day to be alive, sir,' she said cheerfully.

'It is indeed, Mrs Brook.'

7

Alive, he thought grimly as the sudden cool darkness of the interior hallway engulfed him and he climbed the stairs to his study. Beyond the window the distant Pentland Hills glowed in late sunlight. This room containing all his books, his most precious possessions, had never looked more desirable, more comfortable and protective. And he sighed, with an ominous feeling that there might be precious few days like this in the immediate future.

As far as he was concerned, for 'incognito' read 'Royal spy' and he winced at having to conceal his identity. Once a policeman, always a policeman.

That he was incapable of successfully wearing any other disguise was a possibility that Her Majesty obviously had not taken into consideration.

He shuddered as a sudden vision of the Tower of London loomed before him. He had seen gloomy and alarming lithographs of its grim interior and, considering its bloody and dreadful history, it was one place he had no desire to visit either outside or in.

What if he discovered that the Prince of Wales was guilty of worse than cowardice. What then?

The Queen's displeasure for a mission failed and a scandal revealed might at best merit discreet exile to the Colonies, or at worst a rather splendid civic funeral financed by Edinburgh City Police.

Such were his grim thoughts as he prepared to assume the new role necessary for what promised to be a most trying investigation. Given a straight choice, he would have taken on an Edinburgh murder any day.

Chapter 2

'A pity you are no actor,' said Dr Vincent Laurie, who sympathized with his stepfather's present predicament.

For the sake of his two young daughters, Rose and Emily, living in Orkney with their grandmother, Faro realized that he must disregard the Royal Command to the extent of taking a member of his family into his confidence. In case a similar fate awaited him in Elrigg and he too was victim of a mysterious fatal accident.

And who better to be trusted with the details of his secret mission than his stepson whose quick thinking had on many occasions saved his life.

'Elrigg Castle?' said Vince. 'Sir Archie Elrigg's place – equerry to the Prince of Wales, was he not?' Wide-eyed, he looked at Faro. 'The one who has just been gored to death by a bull? A bit about it in the paper few weeks ago. Didn't you read it?'

Faro shook his head rather irritably. He had been particularly busy chasing a notorious villain, a fact that seemed to have escaped his stepson's memory. As he gently reminded him, Vince shook his head.

'The wild cattle are notorious. I seem to remember there was a similar accident in the papers a while back. An actor – Philip Gray. Entertaining guests with monologues from Shakespeare. Remember we saw him in *Hamlet* at the theatre . . .'

As Faro listened, he wondered if the actor had also been the Prince's rival for a lady's love. From the few veiled hints Her Majesty had vouchsafed in this sorry tale

– hints that were all he had in the way of clues – he guessed that Bertie was more than a little interested in the laird's wife, Lady Elrigg, the former actress Miss Poppy Lynne.

Such knowledge was enough to support the theory that Bertie was following the usual pattern of his seductions. Fancy a married lady and, providing the social stratum was correct, the first step on the road to her bed was to appoint her husband as equerry. Next, suggest a weekend shooting party; grouse, deer, wild cattle, nothing on wing or hoof was safe from His Royal Highness's attentions. If the lady was willing and the mansion large enough to conceal indiscretions, the husband was more often than not only too honoured at enjoying Royal patronage to care about being cuckolded.

There were scores of such stories, at least one a year, but for Bertie, Royal sportsman, the thrill was in the kill. Once the lady had succumbed to his arms, the Royal eyes soon wandered. An expensive piece of jewellery for the lady, a knighthood and a bit more land for the husband and there the *affaire* ended. When next the ex-lovers came face to face, a chilly bow of polite acknowledgement was all the lady could reasonably expect to receive for services rendered.

Bertie was always very discreet. Having the husband meet with a particularly nasty accident while his Royal person was on the premises, to say nothing of the publicity such a story might invoke, was clearly most embarrassing.

'What happened exactly?' Vince asked curiously.

'At the moment all I have are some vague theories,' said Faro with a sigh. 'Doubtless I'll have more to tell you when I get back.'

'Wish I could come with you.'

'So do I.'

'Wait a minute. Elrigg's quite near Wooler, isn't it?'

When Faro nodded agreement, Vince said triumphantly, 'I might just be able to look in, see how you're getting on . . .'

The prospect of Vince's presence on any investigation was immensely cheering. Appearances were deceptive, none more than in his stepson's case. Bright curls and a boyishly handsome countenance innocent of guile disguised a keen brain, austere and analytical. Slighter in build than Faro, he was also capable of swift and often deadly movement when danger threatened.

'The Gilchrists have a great aunt who lives near Flodden,' Vince continued. 'She's celebrating her birthday on Saturday and Livvy has hinted once or twice', he added shyly, 'that Great-Aunt would like to meet me and of course, I would love to see the countryside.'

Faro smiled. He had great hopes of Olivia Gilchrist, for this relationship had lasted the best part of a year, much longer than his stepson's usual run of disastrously short-lived courtships. Indeed, he had even developed a sentimental tendency to picture her fondly as Vince's future wife.

The two young people were eminently well suited, Olivia had brains as well as good looks and infinite patience, all excellent qualities for a doctor's wife. There was only one problem that concerned him deeply. Since leaving school she had been tied to her mother's invalid cousin who had brought up Olivia and her twin brother Owen from the age of ten after their missionary parents had died of cholera in India.

When the hitherto strong and active Cousin Edith had been suddenly struck down in late middle age with a mysterious paralysis, Olivia immediately assumed the mantle of dutiful surrogate daughter, self-appointed nurse and companion. Vince assured Faro she did not find this arduous in the least since the two were devoted to each other, with a common love of books and music.

However admirable, such devotion was also the one impediment to his stepson's possible matrimonial intentions. And Faro was forced to accept Vince's claim that this was merely a very dear friendship. Owen and he had been at medical college together and the trio enjoyed a

11

pleasant friendship with no desire for change.

'What precisely are you supposed to be doing at Elrigg?'

'Investigating the disappearance of two paintings the Queen wishes to acquire for her collection . . .'

At the end of his description of the paintings, Faro added helpfully: 'I might take along a magnifying glass, check over their vast collection. Who knows what I might come up with?' he ended cheerfully.

Vince wasn't convinced. 'A bit thin as excuses go, don't you think?'

'I couldn't agree more.' Faro sighed.

'And hardly enough reason for an extended visit.'

'I can take my time about it. I can use your imminent visit as a good reason for lingering in the area, taking a few extra days' holiday. Why not?'

Vince frowned. 'That's all very well but it doesn't guarantee you unlimited access to Elrigg Castle. Besides, you don't know the first thing about art, Stepfather,' he added sternly.

'I know that. Have you any better suggestions?'

Vince was silent. 'Couldn't they have dreamed up something a bit more convincing for your visit, some more plausible excuse?'

'Perhaps Her Majesty isn't rich on imagination – I expect Mr Gladstone had a hand in this one and as far as he is concerned a Royal Command refuses to recognize the impossible. It's all part of the divine right of kings.'

Vince looked at him. 'Of course, the main reason is this so-called accident to Elrigg, I can see that. But why is the Queen so concerned – apart from the anxiety of having the future King of England branded as coward?' he added cheerfully. 'I dare say he'd outlive that one. Royal subjects have short memories, especially for a prince who is also a leader of society.'

'True. But there is a complication. A difference of opinion between Bertie and his equerry – overheard –

angry words in front of the whole castle before they rode out together alone. And only one came back,' he added grimly.

'Bertie?'

'Precisely. He said Elrigg had taken a bad fall from his horse. Help had been summoned on his way back to the castle, the local constable alerted. But when they arrived on the scene, Sir Archie was dead. Not from the fall. Someone had carelessly left a gate open and he had been gored by a bull.'

'Well, that sounds feasible.'

'Except that this was not the first time. On his previous visit to Elrigg, there was a similar incident with a fellow guest—'

'Wait a minute. You aren't saying that he was there when Philip Gray died?'

'I am.'

Vince whistled. 'What a very unfortunate coincidence.' And at Faro's expression, he said slowly, 'You don't surely think he had a hand in it?'

'There was a quarrel certainly – both times.' And Faro frowned again, seeing the damning words of the Prince's letter to his mother.

'In Gray's case, he and Bertie had been playing at cards – for high stakes. Bertie doesn't like to lose and tempers ran high, there were hints at – certain irregularities—'

'Cheating, you mean.'

'Precisely.'

'Gray had a reputation as a gambler,' Vince put in. 'It was well known, I heard about it when he was in Edinburgh . . .'

Ignoring the interruption, Faro continued, 'The two went out alone next morning – Elrigg asked to be excused, indisposed with a bout of toothache. Bertie returned alone. Gray's horse meanwhile had bolted into the high pasture – the domain of the wild cattle. When he didn't return to the castle a search party went out and he was found, gored to death by one of the wild bulls.'

'Very unfortunate. This quarrel between Bertie and Elrigg – what was it about?'

'I have no idea.'

Vince rubbed his chin thoughtfully. 'So you think there is a possible link between the two?'

Faro sighed. 'All I know is guesswork. Gray was young, handsome, adored by the ladies. Perhaps he was also anxious to enjoy Lady Elrigg's favours.'

'A rival, you mean.' Vince sat up in his chair. 'Good Lord – you don't think—'

'I'm trying hard not to – until I know a great deal more, Vince. This is after all circumstantial evidence.'

'Yes, it is. And not very good at that, Stepfather. I can't seriously imagine the heir to the throne killing off his rivals for a lady's favours. After all, with the pick of the field at his disposal, so to speak, would he really care about one more or less drifting towards his bed? As for sullying his hands with murder, surely he has enough influence to discreetly engage someone to do the dire deed for him.'

'Not with his already damaged reputation, Vince.'

'Blackmail, you mean?'

'Precisely. Think of the blackmail potential if the coincidence of these two deaths were made public.'

Vince thought for a moment. 'True. We're in a far from happy position regarding the monarchy. I know he is not popular with his mother's less illustrious subjects, despite that leader of society role.'

As Vince spoke, Faro remembered the Queen's comment: 'If he ever becomes King, he will find all these friends most inconvenient.'

'Running away from an embarrassing situation is a long way from murder, Stepfather,' Vince reminded him.

'Then why didn't he wait for Sir Archie to be brought back home instead of immediately leaving the castle?'

'He did that? How do you know?'

'Because he said so in his letter to the Queen. That was what was worrying him. That he might be thought a

14

coward because he gathered up his entourage. And left immediately.'

'Cut short his visit, you mean?'

'Precisely. "I thought it best to withdraw" – his own words.'

'But he didn't realize that Sir Archie was dead, did he?'

'He might have waited to find out.' And Faro remembered again the whining tones of the spoilt schoolboy. 'Try as hard as I can, Vince lad, this doesn't sound to me like the behaviour of an innocent man.'

'Perhaps the business with the actor made him nervous – it was an appalling coincidence after all.'

Faro looked at him sharply. 'I'm no great believer in coincidences, Vince, and this was altogether too strange. No, it won't do, lad. Think about it. Put yourself in those royal shoes. How would you – or any decent fellow – have reacted had you gone riding with another guest – even one you didn't care for – when you saw him thrown and injured?'

Vince frowned. 'Lacking medical knowledge, I'd have tried to make him comfortable before tearing back for help. And I'd have gone back to direct the rescue party to the spot.'

'Exactly. You wouldn't have rushed back so carelessly that you left the gates open with an injured man lying there and wild cattle in the vicinity.'

Vince shook his head. 'Not unless . . .'

'Unless? You see the doubt. Now you realize what we're dealing with.'

Vince sighed. 'No doubt Bertie will tell you a convincing story. Settle all your fears.'

'I'm afraid not. As you well know, the first place we look for a murderer is within the family circle or close friends, or known enemies, but this is one occasion when I am not allowed to interview the prime suspect.'

'Not allowed – I don't see—'

'Of course you don't. I have been expressly told by Her Majesty that His Royal Highness is not to be interviewed

15

and no mention of his name is to be made. He wishes it kept secret that he was ever at Elrigg at the time of his equerry's death.'

Vince's mouth twisted in distaste. 'All this rather bears out Bradlaugh's scandalous letter, doesn't it?'

The Prince of Wales was twenty-seven in 1868, his behaviour already notorious, when the radical Member of Parliament's sentiments were made public. He wrote, 'This present Prince should never dishonour his country by becoming its King . . . neither his intelligence nor his virtues can entitle him to occupy the throne.'

Vince shook his head. 'I don't envy you this one, Stepfather. A good clean murder would be much more your style.'

As Faro agreed with him, the future of what lay in wait at Elrigg was very fortunately veiled.

Chapter 3

Faro's chief regret as he prepared for a hurried departure from Edinburgh was that he had no time to acquaint himself with the brief of a successful art valuer and investigator. His acquaintance with art was limited to sojourns in the National Gallery as a refuge from the rain or to rest his feet.

His fondness for the Gallery had begun more than twenty years earlier in 1850, when, as a young constable, one of his first assignments had been in the Royal Escort party.

The Prince Consort, turning sharply after the ceremony of laying the foundation stone, momentarily lost his balance. Faro sprang forward, dignity was restored and he was thanked with a warm handshake, a kind word and gentle smile. This was Faro's first encounter with the Royal Family and in one of his weird intuitive flashes he saw a great deal into the character of Prince Albert.

Now, as he headed towards Waverley Station, he wished time had been available to acquire some additional facts about wild cattle. His present rudimentary knowledge was limited to the Highland variety whose menacing horns had cast a terrifying shadow over his childhood holidays with his Aunt Isa on Deeside.

He was still subject to nightmares involving heart-thumping chases which now coloured his mental pictures of the Elrigg herd and he resolved to keep the animals at a safe distance since he disliked all cattle, his distrust extending to the allegedly docile and domestic varieties, such as the dairy cows being led across the meadow past the railway track.

And so, armed with scant knowledge of painters and almost none of cattle, Inspector Faro boarded the southbound Edinburgh train and prepared to emerge at Belford Station transformed into Mr Jeremy Faro, art valuer and insurance investigator.

He had a particular fondness for trains. Had his mind been free from anxiety, he would have enjoyed this opportunity to stare idly out of the window and welcome the inspired avenues of thought that often helped him solve his most difficult cases.

On occasions when the compartment was shared with other passengers, he indulged in a silent game of Observation and Deduction. Sifting through the minute details of their wearing apparel, gestures and habits, he would produce evidence of their stations in life and their reasons for boarding that particular train.

As a boy, Vince had been introduced to this novel game and both had found it an admirable and often hilarious way of passing many an otherwise tedious winter journey.

Today, however, Faro was offered no such diversions. Consumed by anxiety at the prospect ahead, his assumed role was as uncomfortable as an ill-fitting overcoat. Everything seemed to be wrong with it and his misgivings refused to be distracted by the passing countryside.

For once, the beauty of a late-spring day failed to beguile him and he was left quite unmoved by the soft green grass and radiant meadows of the East Lothian landscape. Glimpses of the North Sea, notorious for winter storms, now stretched out to embrace a cloudless horizon radiantly blue and setting forth gentle waves to lap golden beaches with a froth of lace. He remembered his mother's favourite saying: 'God's in his heaven, all's right with the world.'

Had he ever entertained such noble and simple faith, it would certainly have been destroyed by many years of dealing with hardened criminals in a world where neither the guilty nor the innocent were certain of being rewarded by their just deserts.

Earlier dealings with the monarchy had taught him that failure was tantamount to treason in royal eyes and, as for what lay ahead, this might well prove to be the last chapter in his long and faithful employment with the Edinburgh City Police.

If the future King of England was a murderer, or at best, a coward, capable of manslaughter, then Detective Inspector Faro was expendable and his distinguished career would be abruptly and quietly brought to a close.

Trying to shake aside his gloomy thoughts, he realized that his most urgent consideration was how to convince Elrigg Castle of his bogus identity. Perhaps that would be hardest of all, suspecting as he did that his sober dress was inappropriate for anyone connected with the art world.

Catching a glimpse of his reflection in the window, he considered the craggy high-cheekboned face which betrayed his Viking ancestry, the once bright fair hair still thick but now touched with silver.

He sighed. A tall athletic body and deepset watchful eyes told him that his disguise was incomplete. He looked what he was – a policeman, a man of action more accustomed to criminal-catching than browsing idly among valuable paintings.

His dismal preoccupation was interrupted as the train was leaving Berwick Station. Suddenly a porter threw open the door and thrust a young woman into the compartment. Breathless, she threw a coin into the man's hand and as the train gathered speed sat down on the seat opposite.

Faro's sympathetic smile and murmur – 'Well done, well done,' – was dismissed in a single scornful glance.

As the newcomer withdrew a book from her valise and proceeded to read with deep concentration, her attitude presented Faro with a unique opportunity of trying out his Observation game.

Glad of some diversion from his melancholy thoughts, he decided cheerfully that this one was not too difficult. The lady had not come far, for she carried little luggage, only one small travelling bag. Her numerous veils and scarves worn over a cloak of waterproof material indicated that she was used to and prepared for all weathers.

This was confirmed by the condition of her boots, sturdy footwear with scuffed toes, which had seen a good deal of rough walking. She retained hat and gloves so he had no means of seeing hair colour nor of identifying her marital status.

A veiled bonnet concealed most of her face from all but occasional glimpses and her slim figure suggested that she was probably in her early thirties. There Faro knew he was on shaky territory, the first to confess that he usually erred on the side of gallantry where ladies' ages were concerned.

He studied her carefully. Even in the simple matter of reading there was something purposeful and decisive about the way she turned the pages. Here was no nervous, unsure female unused to travelling alone and about to visit a sick relative. She did not look in the least anxious but, suddenly aware of his scrutiny, she looked up from her book and fixed him with a fierce stare.

Embarrassed, he hastily pretended to sleep while continuing to observe, through half-closed eyes, her reflection conveniently provided by the compartment window.

When the train arrived at his destination, he was surprised to see the chilly lady push open the door ahead of him, spring lightly along the platform and claim the hiring cab which Faro soon discovered was the only vehicle the station provided.

One long road disappeared westwards into the hills. According to his map, in that direction lay Elrigg and he leaped forward: 'We are possibly heading in the same direction, madam.'

Head averted, she did not seem to hear him.

He persisted. 'May I be permitted to share your carriage, we appear—'

But before he could explain further, she cut him short with a withering look. 'And where might you be going?'

'To the Elrigg Arms.'

'That is not my destination, I'm afraid. Drive on, if you please,' she instructed the coachman and left Faro standing, staring indignantly after the departing carriage.

Patience was not one of the few virtues he was inclined to boast about and he paced the empty platform angrily, stamping his feet both to relieve his feelings and to keep them warm in the thirty minutes before the cab returned.

He would have been surprised indeed to know that the lady had an ability to observe and deduce that equalled his own.

But for a quite different reason.

She had summed him up accurately as a man without vanity, a man who needed none of the accoutrements of fine clothes and superficial elegance to add false lustre to what nature had given him. And that, she knew from bitter experience, made him all the more dangerous.

Bypassing that strongly male but admittedly attractive and appealing countenance, the straight, slightly hooked nose and the wide-set eyes that, shuddering, she thought resembled those of a bird of prey, she had immediately decided on his identity.

He was a policeman.

A breed of man she hated and feared. One she had learned to recognize, distrust and at all costs avoid.

Chapter 4

The hiring cab returned to the station, collected Faro and the horses set off again at a brisk pace on their uphill climb.

When at last a church spire and a huddle of houses indicated a surprisingly modern town, the coachman pointed with his whip: 'Wooler, sir.'

Faro had heard of Wooler as one of the baronies into which Northumberland was divided after the Norman Conquest. In the twelfth century a rich and prosperous centre of the woollen industry, three centuries later it had borne the full brunt of the Border Wars, with only a hilly mound, a rickle of stones, to mark those turbulent times.

The houses in the main street were newly built and as Wooler disappeared from view the coachman said: 'Almost destroyed by a fire about ten years back, 1862 it was, sir. Second time in less than two hundred years. Even the church over there, see, rebuilt in 1863.'

A short distance from Wooler and the countryside changed dramatically. It was no longer soft and undulating and in front of them rose hills of grimmer aspect. Wild moorland, great crags and huge boulders were the legacy of some ice age when the world was still young.

Now only a few spindly hawthorns taking what shelter they could find suggested that it had seen little in the way of human footsteps or endeavour.

He was acutely aware that he was in an alien land.

Used to the protection of city streets, Faro regarded the scene around him. This was an ancient battlefield which

22

stretched from the Solway Firth to the North Sea, the Debatable Land of history, and he was right in the middle of it.

As if all those ancient bloodthirsty ballads still lived, their battle cries still throbbing to the long and terrible violence that had soaked these hills and moors in blood, for this was the ring in which the champions of England and Scotland clashed arms, some armoured in splendour, proud and valiant, their clansmen running alongside, fighting loyally beside their Border barons. Here the victors robbed, slaughtered and made an end without quarter on either side.

The ballads told it wrong. Many a battle had been lost not by defeat, but by raggle taggle soldiers who seized the chance of pillage while their skins were still intact. With hungry mouths and empty stomachs awaiting their homecoming with the spoils of war, there was no room for sentimental loyalty to lost causes.

To add to Faro's sombre thoughts, the radiant day disappeared to be replaced by clouds hiding the sun. Now he was aware of boulders that moved. A tide of woolly sheep, followed by a shepherd and his dog, signalled a not far distant civilization.

There was something else too, mile upon mile of fences bordered the narrow road.

'We're in the domain of the wild cattle, sir,' the coachman replied to his question. 'They don't like us and we don't like them.'

'Dangerous, are they?'

The coachman laughed uproariously at this naïve question.

'Kill you as soon as look at you, sir. I dare say they feel they have the right to it – the right of way, as you may say. Seeing they were here long before the Romans came. They've seen the killing times come and go – and many a fight that's gone badly for both sides.'

'Could the cattle not have been moved?' he asked.

The coachman thought this was even more humorous than his last question.

'I wouldn't like to try any of that, sir. Wouldn't want their horns in my backside – begging your pardon, sir. Besides, His Lordship says it's best not to interfere with nature ...' He stopped suddenly, remembering that His Lordship had also lost out in the end.

As the road descended once more, Faro felt that the legends and the ballads had never said half enough. They only skimmed the surface of a brutal reality.

The men this land had once supported had lived by the law of the jungle, the same law that saw the survival of the wild cattle hadn't worked for them.

While his beloved Shakespeare was penning the most exquisite prose the world had ever known, or perhaps ever would know, paving the way to an enlightened culture that would last for centuries still unborn, while Elizabethan seamen kept the might of Spain at bay, the monarchs of Scotland and England had emerged from the darkness of the Middle Ages to live in a fair approximation of luxury and culture.

But both were helpless to rule their borders or the men who lived on them. A race apart, their laws were made and their swords wielded by tribal leaders who would have seemed outmoded in the Roman Empire. They were intent on only one thing: the blood feuds, the perennial excuse to annihilate one another.

Not all were peasants, or smallholders, or cattle rustlers. Some were educated gentlemen; a few were peers of the realm. All had in common that they were fighting men of great resource to whom the crafty arts of theft, raid, ambush and sudden death were inborn talents. Men born not with a silver spoon in their mouths but with a steel sword in their hands, the only language they or their enemies understood.

Now time had obliterated all evidence of their savage rule, ancient cruelties and swift death were replaced by a breeze warm and soft about Faro's face. Had this been a social call at Elrigg Castle, he would have looked forward to such a prospect with considerable enjoyment.

Aware that they had travelled for some distance and that in an ever changing skyscape the blue was being overtaken by a steel-like grey, Faro considered how he might tactfully ask the coachman if they were indeed heading in the right direction: 'Is this all the Elrigg estate?'

The coachman pointed to the hilly horizon: 'You'll see the trees first, sir. His Lordship's grandfather was very liberal with trees, planted them everywhere as a protection against the prevailing wind.' And pointing with his whip: 'Look, sir, over yonder.'

The skyline opposite was dominated by a ring of stones. At first glance they looked like the waisted torsos of women petrified in some forgotten dance to gods older than history.

'The headless women, they call them hereabouts,' the driver grinned.

'How charming.'

'You wouldn't say that, sir, at dead of night if you heard them crying.'

'Crying?'

'Aye, sir, that's right. Crying. When the wind's in the right direction,' he added matter-of-factly at Faro's disbelieving expression. 'Acts like organ pipes, though there's others prefer to believe differently.'

His story was cut short by a sudden flurry of rain. As Faro put up the umbrella provided for such an emergency, he was reassured that their destination was almost in sight.

Moments later he was relieved to see a church tower reaching into the sky, followed by a clutter of ancient houses and a twisting ribbon of river. On a hill overlooking the only street, a flag flew from battlements, hinting at the castle which had dominated Elrigg long before the present parkland hid it from the curious.

The Elrigg Arms was a coaching inn of ancient vintage. Time and natural subsidence had thrust its upper storey out of alignment with the lower walls, which also leaned gently but precariously over the paved road.

Instructing the coachman that he would shortly be continuing his journey to the castle, Faro saw his luggage carried into the inn and gave the man a pint of ale for his trouble.

Never willing to waste time on eating, a fact that Vince deplored since it added to his stepfather's tendency to digestive problems, Faro emerged twenty minutes later, reinforced by a rather heavy slice of pie and a dram of whisky.

The coachman, sensing gentry and a larger tip, respectfully tucked a travelling rug about his knees as they resumed their journey. A half-mile up the steep road some dense trees gave way to iron gates and a lodge, which, by its air of neglect and overgrown garden, was unoccupied.

As they sped up the drive, Faro saw that Elrigg Castle was no Gothic edifice, in the current architectural fashion for the romantic but comfortable baronial hall that the Queen had made so popular at Balmoral. Protection from the elements by parkland had been a necessary and wise investment.

Here was the stark realism of a Border peel tower, an oblong bastle house belonging to sterner days when the beasts were kept on the ground floor and in times of stress and danger (which was probably every other Thursday), the inhabitants were rushed in through that high door and the ladder raised so that they could be relatively safe from marauders.

A serious attempt might be made to burn down the tower, but although the laird and his clan would get very uncomfortable underfoot in the process, it was difficult to burn through a solid stone floor. Besides cattle and movable goods were of most interest to raiders, plus any females who happened to be wandering about and could also be carried off.

In the late sixteenth century when the Border was settling down to more peaceful activities, buildings were inclining to comfort first, with a projecting porch and staircase on the outside, three storeyed with small, square headed windows, a ridged roof and embattled parapet.

The tower's original stout doorway, no longer under threat, had been tamed into masquerading as a large and handsome window replacing arrow slits which were now merely picturesque reminders of harsher times.

Ancient oaks now sheltered sheep and a few shy deer who melted into the trees at the carriage's approach. The medieval theme, however, was continued in a field with an archery course from which a young couple had just emerged. Armed with bows and arrows, they were leading their horses through the trees in the direction of the castle.

But they were in no hurry to reach their destination and Faro smiled indulgently. They made an attractive sight; the young man, tall and fair, put his arm about his companion's shoulder and said something that pleased her. Faro heard her laughter as she threw back her head, a gesture that sent her bonnet flying and her light hair rippling over her shoulders.

The young man joined in this peal of merriment, and, leaning over, the girl put out a hand and, patting his cheek, gazed tenderly into his eyes. A moment later they were gone.

Who were they? Dark riding attire did not necessarily indicate mourning relatives. But there was a quality of intimacy about the pair and their mocking laughter that remained with Faro, striking that first incongruous note of warning regarding the house so recently bereaved.

Chapter 5

As the carriage rounded the drive, Faro saw another building crouching alongside the tower, invisible from the drive. Someone had attempted to turn bleak tower into homely mansion by the addition of two storeys, a few windows, a good sprinkling of ivy and not much imagination.

It was set around a square courtyard to house stables and servants, and Faro suspected that it had never seen an architect's plans but had been thrown together by an enthusiastic laird directing an army of loyal tenants who were even less sure of what was required of them. Dwarfed by the original castle, it would have presented no difficulties for any aspiring brigand or determined Border raider.

Faro climbed the steps to the main door, where an ancient butler asked his business and ushered him somewhat breathlessly up a wide stone staircase, considerably worn, not only by many generations of human feet but doubtless by processions of horses and sundry animals.

'If you will wait in here, sir, I will see if Her Ladyship is able to receive you.'

Faro looked around. This then was the Great Hall. A stone fireplace stood at each end, massive enough to have comfortably roasted an ox. The high, vaulted ceiling was of rough stone, as were the walls with sconces for illumination by burning brands or torches. At one end a raised stone dais, for this was the scene of the barony courts where the Elriggs dispensed justice.

And everywhere, suspended as if by magic, a legion of ragged flags from which all colour and delineation had long since vanished. Tributes, he guessed, to every battle that warrior Elriggs of former glory had borne triumphantly from the field.

The sound of light footsteps on stone announced the arrival of Her Ladyship. Her sudden presence was as if the sun had come down to earth.

Later, Faro remembered his quick intake of breath at her radiance. Honey-coloured hair, richly dressed, eyes startlingly blue in a flawless complexion, all enhanced by a jet-encrusted black-velvet gown, which he later described to Vince as fittingly medieval in design.

Expecting the ex-actress to put on a decent performance of Sorrowing Widow, he found instead that he was bowing over the hand of one of the riders he had seen dallying in the grounds, a young woman who exuded warmth and laughter.

When she spoke her voice was resonant with a marvellous cadence, the lyrical quality of pure music. He thought how beautifully she might have played Shakespeare's heroines. She held out hands untouched by that chilly hall, so soft and welcoming that he found himself clinging to them longer than politeness dictated.

The heavy words of condolence he had rehearsed faded. As he stammered them out, she smiled and, as if aware of his embarrassment, she patted his arm gently, as one would offer a small child a gesture of consolation.

'Thank you, sir. I shall miss Archie. He was a kind man.' And, as if that was her last word on the subject, 'I am sure you would like tea, or perhaps something a little stronger. It is a cold, tedious journey from the railway station.'

A tall, thin maid with the same colourless anonymity as the butler appeared silently and put down a tray set for the ritual of afternoon tea.

Faro, invited to sit down opposite Lady Elrigg, prepared to leave the talking to her. A shrewd detective, he knew from experience, can learn a lot about character from apparent irrelevancies. People give much away in trivialities, if one is sharp enough to observe. Gestures too can be revealing.

She talked fondly about the countryside, deplored the weather, loved springtime. There was nothing there for Faro who watched as he listened and had to bite his lip on what he was best at – asking questions.

Suddenly the door opened and the young man, her archery companion, strode in. Faro did not miss the frowning glance the two exchanged, a warning from Lady Elrigg could not have been more clearly expressed if the words had been shouted across the room.

Then smiling, calm, she was introducing Faro to the newcomer.

'This is Mark, Archie's stepson.'

'My mother was an Elrigg cousin,' Mark explained.

As they shook hands, Faro realized that not only were the years between the two less than a decade but also that they brought into that bleak cold hall a substantial aura of affection and intimacy, which they made no attempt to conceal.

If this was illicit love, was that devotion strong enough for murder? Oh yes, Faro knew it was. He had learned through twenty-five years of criminal cases, that love was the strongest of human passions, one ruthlessly to stamp out ties of blood and duty. From the dawn of history man had been fully aware of its potential long before Cain destroyed his brother Abel.

Frowning, Lady Elrigg handed Mark the card which had been hastily printed for Faro in Edinburgh.

'Mr Faro's here about the missing pictures, Mark,' she added rather loudly with a slight emphasis on the words.

Mark opened his mouth but, before he could speak, she said, still smiling: 'Archie apparently told the insurance assessors – this gentleman's people – that the pictures were missing.'

And to Faro: 'This is all rather a surprise to us.'

It was indeed, thought Faro, for Mark continued to look not only surprised but quite dumbfounded.

Taking up the theme of the missing paintings and hoping to sound businesslike and convincing, Faro had a very nasty moment as Mark, studying the card, looked at his stepmother and said sharply: 'He never mentioned any insurance people to me.'

Lady Elrigg shook her head and smiled at Faro. She did not seem in the least perturbed that the paintings had not yet been recovered and her manner of indifference confirmed Faro's own growing suspicion.

'I can show you the place where they used to hang, if you like. There is still a mark on the wall.' She laughed as he and Mark followed her upstairs into the dining room with its massive refectory table stretching the entire length of the room.

As they entered, from every wall the faces of ancestral Elriggs glared down at them. Expressions of arrogance, suspicion, mild astonishment and rarely any degree of pleasure suggested that the steely-eyed glances of these ancient warlords might have set the digestion of sensitive diners at a disadvantage.

'Over here.' Lady Elrigg pointed to the space between several sporting prints of indifferent merit and two large unhappy landscapes suggesting that Northumberland existed in the eternal gloom shed by a forest of Caledonian pines.

Faro pursed his lips obligingly and stared at the blank wall in what he hoped was the manner of an insurance assessor giving his subject deep and earnest thought and doing a careful assessment by a process of mental arithmetic.

Poppy Elrigg helped him out. 'I can't help you, I'm afraid I know absolutely nothing about paintings, valuable or otherwise. The one of old King George was of historic importance, I expect, but he was such a clown – all that ridiculous tartan on such a figure.' Her giggle was infectious, looking from one to the other, inviting them to abandon their sober expressions and join in her mirth.

When they continued to watch her, solemn as owls, she added, 'I suppose the one of the Prince of Wales with his foot on one of our wild bulls could possibly be of some value, of course – to anyone who had a personal concern.'

Faro looked at her quickly. Did she know of the Queen's interest?

Again she shrugged, a dismissive but elegant gesture. 'If a painting or an ornament is pretty and it pleases me, whether it cost a few pence or a few thousand pounds, well, that's all I care about. But Archie was different. Valuable things were his domain. He was so knowledge-able, a great collector. We have attics full of the weirdest assortment that took his fancy from every place he visited, I imagine, all over the world.'

Pausing, she smiled at them, her sidelong glance impish. 'He couldn't resist beautiful things.' Her lip curled gently as, pretty as any picture, she added slowly, 'And he was prepared to pay a great deal for what he wanted, you know. One could say beauty was an obsession with him.'

She gave Faro a slightly arch glance, daring him to come to his own conclusions about that strange marriage and, turning from the empty spaces above them, she laughed again, that echoing sound at once carefree and infectious and totally inappropriate for a wife so recently bereaved.

Unhampered by her voluminous skirts, she walked quickly ahead of them, long-legged and graceful, moving her hands in light gestures as she talked. She was, thought Faro admiringly, a sheer delight for any man to watch.

'The police were notified, I expect Archie told them, or you wouldn't be here,' she said, her quick glance demanding confirmation.

As he nodded vaguely, Mark muttered agreement. 'Yes, of course. Talk to them.' He sounded suddenly eager, relieved to shed any responsibility for the pictures' disappearance.

When his stepmother said nothing, leading the way towards the great hall, he fell into step after them mutely. But glancing suspiciously at Faro his manner was loyally protective, indicating that should this strange man

32

threaten her in any way, he was ready to spring to her assistance.

Suddenly apologetic, Poppy Elrigg turned to Faro: 'We should have made more of it, I know, but then . . . the accident – you know . . .' Her voice trailed off.

'The very next day. Put everything else right out of our minds,' said Mark with a glance of stern reproach in Faro's direction as Lady Elrigg took out a lace handkerchief and sniffed into it dutifully.

Faro, watching the touching scene, murmured sympathetically and prepared to take his leave.

'I shall be staying at the Elrigg Arms for several days, while my inquiries continue. My stepson is arriving at the end of the week, we plan to spend a few days walking. Presumably my business will be finished by then.'

The two listened to him glumly, their faces expressionless, their minds clearly elsewhere.

He had to go. There was nothing else for it. He could hardly expect to be invited to supper. A mourning widow, that lace handkerchief being twisted in delicate fingers was a reproach, a reminder of her grief which provided a very good excuse for terminating the interview.

In a last stab at politeness, she smiled wanly, offering the pony trap to take him back to his hotel.

He declined, saying that he preferred to walk. Their relief at his departure was so obvious he guessed that they were even less happy in their roles of grieving kin than he was at presenting himself as a noteworthy and really reliable insurance assessor of valuable works of art.

Walking briskly down the drive, he went carefully over the scene he had just left. What evidence, if any, had been revealed during that brief meeting?

First, and most important, he had seen enough to know that Sir Archie had left no grieving spouse and that some powerful emotion existed between his stepson and his young widow.

As for the paintings, their disappearance during the

Prince's visit confirmed Faro's earlier suspicions. Poppy Elrigg's statement that her late husband was obsessive about possessions had a certain kinship to the childlike greed that was one of the Queen's characteristics. As far as Her Majesty was concerned, merely to comment, to enthuse aloud, was to demand.

Did her son also believe in the divine right of kings to their subjects' goods and chattels? Was he on the wrong track and had the Prince's quarrel with his equerry been a wrangle over two paintings of indifferent merit but of sentimental value to Her Majesty?

Most important of all, what was the relationship between the Prince and Lady Elrigg? He would need to know a great deal more about the stage that had reached before he could set the scene with accuracy. One would have imagined that the recent Mordaunt divorce might have given the Prince reason for caution, especially when he was named in Sir Charles's petition against his twenty-one-year-old wife. Lady Mordaunt had thereupon tearfully confessed that she had 'done wrong with the Prince of Wales and others, often and in open day'.

The press had leaped with joy upon such a scandal and the Prince's letters had been printed in *The Times*. There were many prepared to read very diligently between the lines of what appeared to be simple gossipy letters and come to conclusions that did little to enhance the Royal reputation.

Faro sighed. In common with that other less fortunate royal family, the Bourbons, it seemed that the Saxe-Coburgs learned nothing and forgot nothing.

Chapter 6

The supper room at the Elrigg Arms sported ancient oak beams, dark panelling and a regiment of antlers as well as an assortment of glass-entombed tiny animals. Their bright eyes followed Faro as he walked across a floor on which only the sturdiest of tables could rest all four legs at the one time.

A cheerfully cracking log fire shed a glow of welcoming hospitality but any hopes Faro had of meeting fellow diners inclined to local gossip were doomed to failure. The two gentlemen who shared one end of the oak refectory table greeted him politely and hastily resumed a conversation that revealed them as business acquaintances travelling north to Edinburgh.

Another diner entered. The chilly lady from Faro's railway encounter. As her presence suggested she was also staying at the inn, he felt a resurgence of indignation that she had deliberately left him standing on the station platform when they might have shared the only hiring carriage.

Her brief acknowledgement of his cold bow declined admission of any earlier meeting. Firmly opening the book she carried indicated to her fellow diners that she intended keeping her own counsel.

Despite her formidable attitude, the lamplit table revealed what veils and scarves had kept hidden, an abundance of dark auburn hair and slanting green eyes, which suggested in her less disagreeable moments capabilities of appeal, even enticement.

Observing the secret glances exchanged by the two other gentlemen, Faro decided that such looks might encourage the attentions of predatory males and that her chilly reception was perhaps a necessity for a female travelling alone.

As the plates were passed round he observed ink-stained fingernails. An artist or some clerkly occupation, school teacher or governess? Even as he pondered, she wasted no time over eating but tackled each course in a hearty businesslike manner, far from the polite toying with food in public that characterized genteel members of her sex. Eager to be gone, with a murmured excuse she rose from the table so abruptly that the capacious leather bag she carried slid to the floor and disgorged a quantity of papers.

As Faro helped her to retrieve them, they were snatched from his hands, with hardly a word of thanks. He sat back in his chair and realized that he had been correct in his suspicions. Such rudeness, however, was inexcusable. He hoped he had seen the last of this formidable travelling lady as he devoted his attention to the increased buzz of voices that issued from the public bar.

There might be valuable information to be obtained regarding his mission by mingling with the tenants and he carried through his pint of ale.

A few farmers were playing cards and although his greeting was politely received by no stretch of imagination could it be called encouraging. It was neither as warm nor even as mildly curious as the flurry of tail-wagging the scent of a stranger stirred among their farm dogs.

He patted a few heads and distributed liberal 'good fellow's but this failed to play him into their owners' confidences. Resolutely they devoted themselves again to their game, having called their fraternizing animals sternly to order.

Refusing to be daunted, Faro threw in some cheerful remarks about good weather, to be greeted by grunts and at most a few disbelieving headshakes. He had almost given up hope of any success and was about to retreat to his room when the door opened.

The man who entered was clad in an indescribably dirty, voluminous greatcoat which contained more than his large frame and Faro realized he was face-to-face with the local poacher. The huge garment wrapped tentlike about him was composed of inside pockets large enough comfortably to stow away a variety of game birds and small animals for the pot and, by the smell of it, included an interesting range of fish.

Faro's greeting to the newcomer was cordially but toothlessly received, its warmth strengthened by the offer of a jug of ale. The poacher's eyes glistened and he responded cheerfully to Faro's careful overtures about the weather for the time of year.

'Travelling in this area are you, sir?'

'Briefly,' said Faro.

'Fisherman, are you?'

'Alas, no.'

The poacher regarded him, head on side. 'Naught much for a gentleman to do, to fill in his time, like.'

Refusing to be drawn and hoping to direct the conversation towards the castle, Faro asked: 'I presume there is much casual employment hereabouts during the shooting season?'

'Just for the young lads, the beaters. But I'd never let one of my lads go – dead dangerous it is, those high-nosed gentry are awful shots,' he added confidentially. 'Few years back, there was one killed . . .'

'What are you going on about, Will Duffy?' The enquiry came sharply from the barman who had edged his mopping-up activities on the counter a shade nearer. 'That was an accident,' he said sharply to Faro. 'Such things do happen.'

'Mebbe,' was the poacher's reply. 'Mebbe like the horns over yonder.' So saying he nodded towards a bull's head among the decapitated trophies adorning one wall.

Caring little for the present bloodthirsty fashion in

37

wall decoration, Faro had given this evidence of sporting skill scant attention. Now he observed for the first time that the splendid white bull's head lacked horns.

'You probably know more than most about what happened to them,' the barman said heavily to Duffy, who thereupon leaned across the counter, his fists bunched in a threatening manner: 'Are you saying that I pinched them, Bowden?'

'It wouldn't be the first time something had gone a-missing from my walls . . .'

Duffy stood up to his full height, bulging pockets giving him monumental stature.

'Are you accusing me?' he said in menacing fashion.

Faro and the other drinkers stood by, fascinated by what promised to be a fists-up between barman and poacher, men of equal height and weight.

'Duffy!' At that moment the door behind them was flung open and an elderly man with the look of a prosperous farmer glared in. 'Gossiping again, are you? Am I to wait all night while you fill yourself with drink?'

'Coming, sir.'

The poacher, suddenly deflated, tipped Faro an embarrassed wink and allowed himself to be meekly led away.

'When did this happen?' Faro asked Bowden, nodding towards the bull's head.

'A while back. Duffy can't keep his hands off anything that might fetch a few pennies.' And, refusing to be drawn into any further conversation with a stranger, the barman returned to polishing the counter as if his life depended on a shining, stain-free surface.

Faro's bedroom boasted a cheery fire and a large four-poster bed, plus the uneven floor of antiquity which creaked at every step. His door added to this orchestra of rheumatic boards. Testing the bed gingerly, he was pleased to find that the mattress was of a more modern vintage than the faded velvet canopy and ragged, brocade curtains.

Drawing the oil lamp closer, he took out his notebook and logged the day's events, ending: 'Wild bull's horns missing from public bar. Duffy might know something about the Elriggs and be willing to talk for a fee? Talk to him again!'

He slept well that night and awoke to the appetizing smell of ham and eggs. He was relieved to find that his digestion was not hampered by the presence of the chilly lady at the breakfast table, and ten o'clock was striking on the church clock as he walked down the main street.

Between post office and barber's shop, a one-time cottage bore on its window the words POLICE STATION. A narrow hallway ended in a door with a heavy bolt and a heavily barred square cut out of the central panel. It might serve as an imposing warning to the local inhabitants, but Faro doubted whether it had ever held a criminal with violent inclinations and uncongenial habits.

Opening the door marked ENQUIRIES. PLEASE ENTER, he stepped into what had once been the parlour. A large desk sat uneasily against one wall while a wooden form opposite offered uncomfortable seats for inquirers.

The constable on duty had the healthy look of an elderly countryman who has had a good life: white-haired, apple-cheeked and overweight. He nodded in reply to Faro's question and pointed to the closed door.

'It's Sergeant Yarrow you'll be wanting, sir. He has a visitor – if you'll just take a seat.'

Pondering on the hierarchy of two policemen in charge of a village station, Faro heard men's voices raised angrily from behind the half-glassed door on the other side of the room.

'You'd better do something about it, then.' The first voice was cultured, authoritative.

'I'm doing all I can—' The second voice was slow, weary.

'Which isn't half good enough. I demand permission to excavate the site,' was the reply.

'I cannot grant that. You know perfectly well it was refused by your late uncle—'

'Who is happily no longer with us,' said the first man, cutting short the weary man's shocked exclamation. 'It was just his pig-headedness after all, his sense of possession. Scared that I might find treasure trove or some such nonsense. And, dammit, on what is, if there was any justice left in this country, my own land after all.'

'Look, sir,' there was an attempt at mollification in the other speaker's voice. 'Not a bit of use going on like this. I know you have a right to feel resentment, but the police can't help you here. It's lawyers – good ones – you're needing.'

'Lawyers, you say. I've wasted years trying to prove my inheritance. I've lived in a cramped, damp cottage when my rightful place should have been up there – in the castle. Damn you, man, you know all this, you know how unjust he's been, but you're on his side. He bought the law just as he bought everything else.'

The other man's protest was cut short by a sound suspiciously like a fist thumping a table followed by a crash.

The constable regarded Faro nervously, suspected that this scene was making a bad impression and decided to intervene. Taking the law into his own hands, he marched to the closed door and rapped loudly on it.

'Visitor to see you, Sergeant.'

The door opened and, with a final curse, a young man exploded into the office and vanished out of the hallway.

'I seem to have come at an awkward time,' said Faro, aware that his words were a masterpiece of understatement.

Sergeant Yarrow did not rise to greet him. Perhaps this was due to the vexation caused by the angry young man's hasty exit, but Faro felt that his reception was less than cordial.

Closer to Faro in age than the constable at the desk, he did not look nearly as fit. There was nothing of the rosy-cheeked countryman about his sallow complexion and heavily lined face. Only his eyes were remarkable, a bright pale blue with the iris clearly defined.

As Faro introduced himself in his assumed role, he realized that the sergeant must once have possessed outstanding good looks with such eyes and black curling hair, now thin and grey.

Even as he wondered what suffering had brought about this premature ageing, with a weary sigh Yarrow began impatiently ruffling the papers on his desk, his gesture indicating that such callers as Mr Jeremy Faro were wasting his time.

Put out by his attitude, Faro was almost tempted to reveal his true identity but thought better of it instantly. The whole point of his mission was to remain incognito. An insurance investigator was within his rights to interview the policeman who had examined the deceased after the accident and talk to the doctor who had signed the death certificate.

'Was there a coroner's inquest?'

Yarrow stared at him. 'Of course. A verdict of accidental death was recorded. You had better talk to Constable Dewar about it,' he added sharply, eyeing his piles of paper as if straining to get back to really important business. 'He has all the details and can let you see the statements.'

So saying, the sergeant stood up to speed this tiresome time-wasting enquirer on his way. As he walked across the floor, Faro observed that he was lame and that the effort cost him some discomfort.

He decided he would like to know a lot more about the Elrigg Police and their curious hierarchy.

Chapter 7

Constable Dewar's reception of Mr Jeremy Faro, insurance assessor, was considerably more encouraging than that of Sergeant Yarrow. His eyes brightened, his eagerness to be helpful confirmed Faro's suspicions of a daily round with nothing more exciting than stranded animals or pursuit of the local poacher.

Faro produced an official-looking notebook and said he wished to be taken to the scene of Sir Archie Elrigg's demise. Dewar regarded this activity with nervous anxiety. His eyes widened on being informed that this was the usual procedure when violent death was involved to which there had been no witnesses.

'Coroner said there were no suspicious circumstances, if that's what you're inferring, sir. And he is His Lordship's cousin,' Dewar added indignantly, his tone implying that such an eminent member of the family could not be in question on points of law.

'Besides,' he continued, 'I'd have never thought the family would need things like insurance, what with all their wealth. Death insurances seem to be only for common folk like us.' With a sigh, he added, 'Aye well, ye live and learn.'

'We do indeed. The site of the accident – is it far?'

'No, sir, but we can drive there.' Dewar stood up. 'If you'll follow me.'

The police vehicle turned out to be a pony trap. As they jogged up the hill at a leisurely pace, with an ancient

42

horse who, Faro decided, would be as inept as the constable at pursuing a fleeing criminal, he used the opportunity to satisfy his curiosity regarding the Elrigg constabulary.

'Do you see a great deal of crime?'

Dewar laughed merrily at such a ridiculous idea. 'What – here? Not on your life. The local poacher keeps us busy and that's about all.'

'I should have imagined that an experienced constable like yourself would be all that was needed to keep order.'

'Indeed that was the case. Sergeant Yarrow came to us from the Metropolitan Police Force a few years back. Very badly shot up in one of their murder hunts. Cornered the villains, single-handed. Got an award for it,' he added proudly, 'but he was finished for active service.'

Dewar sighed. 'End of a promising career. Refused to retire. Asked for a quiet country posting up north, where he came from. His Lordship thought highly of him although he was appointed by the Northumberland Constabulary.'

'Isn't that the usual procedure?' Faro asked.

Dewar shook his head. 'His Lordship has the last word, makes the decisions. Only right and proper, since it is his property we are looking after. However, the Sergeant was personally recommended by the Chief Constable, who is kin to Sir Archie.'

Before Faro could comment, Dewar continued. 'Old wounds plague him a bit, poor fellow. But he's a good just man, well liked and respected by everyone.'

And a good man to have around, thought Faro, if it's a murder we're investigating. An experienced officer I can trust should an emergency arise.

They had reached the summit of the hill where the landscape was once more dominated by the weird stone circle.

Faro pointed to it. 'Interesting?'

'The headless women, sir,' said Dewar.

'I can see the reason for that. They look like sawn-off torsos.'

43

'Some say they were Celtic princesses, five sisters. Decapitated by the Romans and turned into stone.' Dewar chuckled. 'You should hear them crying, sir. When the wind's in the north, it echoes through the gulleys and channels. Makes your blood run cold to hear it.'

Faro looked back towards the village nestling peaceful and serene at the base of the hill. Smoke from its peat fires climbed wraithlike into the still air.

Constable Dewar smiled at him. 'Folk hereabouts believe the old superstition that the headless women are calling for vengeance.'

Between the standing stones and the road a line of trees marched sharply downwards to a grass-covered plateau.

'That's the old hillfort, sir,' said Dewar. 'Just below – see, there's the wild cattle.'

Distant white shapes grazed peacefully about three hundred yards and one substantial fence away as Faro descended from the pony trap whose ancient horse was being sympathetically patted by Dewar.

'Out of breath, old fellow? You take a good rest now.'

What would Superintendent McIntosh make of the Elrigg Police and their archaic mode of transport, thought Faro, used to the swift well-trained horses of the Edinburgh City Police, drawing the police carriage as it rattled across the cobblestones of the High Street, striking fear into the hearts of its citizens as it carried the guilty to justice?

Following Dewar to the site of the accident, keeping a watchful eye on the empty, bleak pastureland that lay between the cattle and the safety of the road they had just left, he was relieved to set foot inside the only shelter offered, a tiny copse of birch trees and bushes.

'The Elrigg shooting parties go mainly for game birds, foxes and the like,' the constable explained. 'Occasionally the guests are allowed to kill some of the wild cattle, if numbers have to be kept down, that is.'

Safe within the copse, Faro breathed again.

'They look just like an ordinary herd of cows,' he said.

Dewar nodded. 'You don't see many all-white herds, sir. When you get closer you'll see they're very different, smaller than our beef and dairy cattle. And with those horns,' he laughed, 'a lot more dangerous.'

Suddenly sober, remembering their mission, he said quietly: 'This is where I found His Lordship. There's the gate that was left open. That's how the beast got in at him.'

'A moment, Constable. Can we go back to the beginning, if you please? Two gentlemen out riding, one of them is thrown by his horse. His companion suspects he is badly injured, goes for help . . .'

As he spoke, Faro's brief examination of the gate revealed a sturdy heavy iron latch which could hardly have been left open accidentally. Except by someone leaving in too much of a panic to check that it was closed, he thought grimly.

'Am I correct, so far?'

Dewar grinned. 'You are, sir. As luck would have it Sergeant Yarrow and I were out riding on duty together that day. We need the horses when we have a lot of ground to cover during the shoot. We are expected to keep an eye on things. The Sergeant being lame and I'm not a young man any more, we both move fairly slowly on foot.'

'You usually accompany a shooting party?'

'That's correct, sir. Oversee it, in case of accidents.'

'But there wasn't a shooting party that day?'

Dewar looked uncomfortable. 'No, but there had been earlier that week. You see, at the Castle they were entertaining a very special guest, an important gentleman.' He went on hurriedly before Faro could ask if he knew this important gentleman's identity. 'We had also been warned to keep a lookout for those two valuable paintings that went missing.'

Faro had no wish to be diverted from the circumstances

45

of Archie's death. He had already decided that there had been no burglary at the castle. And that the paintings had been conveniently stored away by the Elriggs themselves, safe from Her Majesty's acquisitiveness.

'Did you witness the accident by any chance?'

'No. But we were just a short distance away – over there, on the pastureland when the gentleman rode over to us. He was in a dreadful state. A real panic. Said he was going for help.'

'Were the cattle about?'

'Oh yes, they were grazing. Just like today.'

'And you rode among them?'

'Not quite among them, sir, that would be asking for trouble. We kept at a safe distance and if you're on horseback they don't attack. Seems as if they only see the horses and don't consider other four-footed creatures as their enemies. It's odd because they don't seem aware of the men on their backs.'

'And what happened then?'

'Sergeant Yarrow told me to ride like the devil for the doctor and bring back the pony trap from the station in case we needed it to carry Sir Archie back if he was badly injured. He'd stay with him meantime, see if there was anything he could do to help.'

'How long did all this take?'

Dewar shook his head. 'I didn't take much notice of time to tell truth, sir. I was a bit flustered – His Lordship injured and all that. We're not used to crises like that. I suppose we thought of Sir Archie as being immortal. A bit like God. And he wasn't the sort that accidents happen to, could ride like the wind, drunk or sober.'

He was silent for a moment. 'I had to tell Her Ladyship and get old Clarence ready for the pony trap.' He sucked his lip, calculating. 'I'd reckon I was away nearly an hour at least. When I got back Dr Brand was already there with Sergeant Yarrow. And I knew, just by looking at their faces, that it was too late.'

Dewar stopped and glanced at Faro who was studying

the ground curiously. 'Is there something wrong, sir?'

'Has there been much rain since the accident?'

Dewar clearly thought this an odd question. 'Not more than a few showers, sir. We're having a dry spell.'

Kneeling down, Faro examined the ground, ran the soil through his fingers, but any evidence had long since returned to dust. A few weeks was enough to obliterate the churned-up mud which might have preserved evidence of two riders side by side, and even of a charging animal.

Dewar watched, too polite to ask the burning questions brought about by such strange behaviour.

Faro straightened up, smiled at him. 'Footprints and horses' hoofs, sharp and clear, can tell us a lot. Did you notice anything unusual?'

And when Dewar looked merely puzzled, Faro pointed: 'About the ground, I mean.'

Dewar thought for a moment. 'Odd that you should ask, sir.' And rubbing his chin thoughtfully, 'When I came back with the others, I walked around – ' He grinned. 'Just the policeman in me, sir. Can't help that. And when the doctor said Sir Archie had been gored, I wondered about the bull's hoofprints.'

'There were some?'

'No, sir, that's what was odd. There weren't any. Nothing to indicate the churned-up ground a great heavy angry beast would make charging down on someone.'

'Did you point it out to Sergeant Yarrow?'

Dewar looked embarrassed. 'Yes, I did. But he wasn't impressed. I don't blame him,' he added hastily. 'He's a city policeman really, and they don't see things like country folk born and bred. Besides,' he added reluctantly, 'he does make a bit of fun of me, says I'm always on the lookout, hoping for a crime but that I'd never recognize one if it stared me in the face.'

His voice was sad, then he laughed. 'He's probably right, sir. Crimes are the last thing he wants. And you can understand that, after all he's been through he values a

47

peaceful life above all things. Not like me, I've never had much chance of real crime,' he added in tones of wistful regret.

Faro smiled. Such reaction fitted in with Yarrow's relaxed attitude to crime, however, if Dewar's observations were correct, the omission of hoofprints should have perturbed him considerably. He said consolingly: 'Well, you were quite right to bring it to Sergeant Yarrow's attention, even the smallest thing can be of importance.'

'I could have been wrong, I admit that. The rescue party from the castle with horses and the like would have covered up any other tracks.'

He paused, looking back towards the village, remembering. 'I told Her Ladyship. She was very upset and there was a great deal of bustle in the house. Maids rushing this way and that. The other gentleman, the one with the beard, that had been riding with His Lordship, he was leaving. He seemed to be in a great hurry.'

Dewar shook his head, at a loss to know how to continue but with condemnation in every line of his face. 'A very important guest, he was,' he said heavily. Again he hesitated, aware that Faro was a stranger, then he continued: 'As you maybe know, sir, His Lordship is – was – equerry to the Prince of Wales. You'd have thought in the circumstances he'd have waited . . .'

His lip curled scornfully, indicating more than any words, his contempt for this very important guest who did not even stay long enough to see Sir Archie carried home, to comfort his bereaved family and respectfully see him laid to rest.

Did Dewar know the identity of the bearded gentleman? It was quite outside the strict purpose of police procedure laid down for the protection of royalty for the local police not to be informed of the Prince's incognito. It indicated that the Northumberland Constabulary treated such visitors much more casually than the Edinburgh City Police, where royalty brought safety measures to a fever pitch of activity.

Presumably Sergeant Yarrow had been lulled into a false sense of security by the Chief Constable being kin to the laird and subscribed to the view that in this remote village outside time, where the Elriggs ruled supreme, assassins and murderers never lurked.

Chapter 8

As he followed Constable Dewar across the field, Faro noticed on the other side of the copse an area roped off on the raised plateau with evidence of an archaeological dig.

'That's Mr Hector Elrigg's domain,' Dewar told him.

Faro looked at him. 'Another Elrigg?'

'Sir Archie's nephew,' said Dewar, and continued, 'the old hillfort was built long before the Romans came – or anyone else for that matter. Except the cattle, of course – they were roaming about long before men set foot in the Cheviots. Mr Hector's been digging for years. I think he's hoping for buried treasure . . .

'Claims that all this is rightly his, that his father was tricked out of his inheritance. Not to put too fine a point on it, sir, it was all wine, women and gambling with Mr Malcolm, the young Master of Elrigg. He was not a good man,' said Dewar reluctantly, 'and he'd have gone to prison and the estate sold, if it hadn't been for Mr Archie, his younger brother.

'Mr Archie was completely different. As he didn't expect to inherit the title he'd gone off and built up a fine shipping line in Newcastle. He paid off all his brother's debts, but Mr Archie was a keen business man and the price was high – Elrigg was to be turned over to him – and his heirs.

'No one believed that Mr Malcolm would agree to such terms, but agree he did. He signed the document, took a boat out at Alnmouth and was never seen again. Mr Hector feels bitter about it. A man can understand that.

Having to lose his rightful inheritance, in payment of his father's sins.'

As the village came in sight, Dewar asked: 'Where shall I set you down, sir?'

'I'll come back with you, if I may, and have a word with Sergeant Yarrow.'

'As you please, sir.'

'What can I do for you, Mr Faro?'

Sergeant Yarrow smiled, his greeting friendly and, as he indicated a seat opposite, Faro decided that their first meeting must have taken him at a bad moment, his calm ruffled by the stormy interview with Hector Elrigg.

'Has Dewar been helpful?'

'Indeed he has. We have just returned from the site of the accident.'

Yarrow nodded. 'And he gave you a report on what happened?'

'He did. There are just a few questions which you might be able to answer, sir.' Faro paused and Yarrow nodded agreement.

'Of course, I'll be glad to help, if I can.'

'Sir Archie was already dead when you reached him?'

'Alas, yes, I was too late.'

'What did you think when you examined the body, Sergeant?'

'That he hadn't been lying there very long. Perhaps half an hour. After sending Dewar off for help, I didn't reach the copse as fast as I intended. My damned horse went lame and I had to lead her the last part – very cautiously I can tell you, with the cattle roaming about.

'Fortunately I knew exactly where to find him. The copse is the only bit of shelter this side of the hill. But the gentleman's directions were very precise, considering the state he was in. White as a sheet and very upset he was. Almost in tears.'

He sighed. 'Alas, by the time I got there, it was too late. There was no sign of Sir Archie's horse. The cattle – they

51

were grazing nearby – and someone, presumably the gentleman in his panic, had left the gate open.'

'And you think a bull had been attracted by the noise and had charged the man on the ground?'

Even as Faro said the words, he found such a statement most unlikely. The beast, he thought, was more likely to have been scared off . . .

'You see, sir, the old bull, the king bull, would be enraged by the blood, they smell blood – and fear, too, so I'm told.'

'Blood? I didn't know Sir Archie was bleeding.'

Yarrow shook his head. 'Not His Lordship's blood – his own. Dewar probably mentioned that there had been a shoot earlier in the week. It happens from time to time when guests who want a shoot come to the castle. It was the same procedure as in olden times, until lately. Like a hunt in the Middle Ages.'

'What do they use? Bows and arrows?' Faro asked in amazement.

'That's right, sir. And crossbows. And everyone comes, a regular festival with a feast afterwards. A notice goes up that a wild bull will be killed on a certain day. The men – and some of the women too – come on horse and foot and then the horsemen ride off the bull that's the intended target.'

'Ride him off?'

'Yes, try and get him away from the rest of the herd. And when he stands at bay, the chief marksman, usually His Lordship or the most honoured guest, dismounts and fires the first arrow. That goes on until the old bull succumbs. You can imagine that the old fellow gets wilder and wilder, in pain as he is.'

'I can imagine,' said Faro sourly.

Yarrow gave him a quick glance. 'I – see you don't approve, sir. No more than I do. I'm a town man myself but in the country these traditions are hard to break. Everyone comes along who is capable of shooting an arrow, even little bairns. The Elrigg family are born to it.

Experts – Mr Hector and Mr Mark were trained from when they could first hold a bow.'

He paused and smiled proudly. 'Everyone is encouraged to take up the local sport and I'm now quite a good marksman myself, so is Dewar. But I prefer to stick to the archery field. We'll be having our annual contest – for the Golden Arrow – next week.'

'Really. With the castle in mourning?'

'Her Ladyship's decision. She said Sir Archie would have wanted everything to go on as normal. He would have wished to have the contest and not disappoint all the tenants.'

'That was very far seeing of her,' said Faro as he wondered at her motives.

'Come if you can. You'll be most welcome. The proceeds go to the Elriggs' favourite charities.'

'I doubt whether I'll be here then. With all these arrows flying about it might be a dangerous pastime for an observer.'

Yarrow frowned. 'The bull slaying was – for some. Not always fatal but like the ones used in the Spanish bullfights, they could turn very nasty. And that was when Sir Archie's grandfather decided most humanely that the beast should be finished off by rifle fire.'

'And that was what happened last week?'

'Yes. But some of them are not very good on the guns . . .'

He was silent, frowning before he continued: 'They thought they wounded one, but not the king bull. They were probably wrong and if His Lordship wasn't dead in the fall, and struggling to get to the road, the bull might have seen and set about him with his horns. It looked to me like that was the case—'

'What makes you think that?'

'He was gored in the back.' He shrugged away the unpleasant picture. 'And that was the end of him.'

Again he fell silent, his face bleak, his expression harsh with suffering. And Faro remembered that Yarrow had seen many deaths and had almost lost his own life.

'Did you see anyone else in the area – who could have helped perhaps?'

Yarrow regarded him curiously. 'Not in the immediate vicinity,' he said heavily.

'But near enough?' said Faro eagerly.

He looked away. 'Hector Elrigg, Sir Archie's nephew. You – almost – met when you came to the station,' he added with a wry grimace. 'When I found Sir Archie, Hector was working at the hillfort.' He drew a deep breath. 'I shouted to him for help . . .'

'And – ' said Faro softly.

Yarrow gave him a glance of desperate appeal. 'Look, there is probably nothing in this at all. I just didn't care for his attitude. He was rather flippant about the whole thing. A downright refusal, sir, that's what I got from Hector Elrigg,' he added in shocked tones.

'From what you heard when you arrived earlier on, you'll realize he's a difficult sort of young devil, but I try to be fair-minded. And I'm certainly not suggesting that Hector seriously wished his uncle dead or would have tried to bring it about. Not at all.'

Wondering whether he should have revealed his true identity to Yarrow, Faro returned to the inn. In the empty bar he had a good look at the bull's magnificent de-horned head and decided that in life he must have been an ugly customer to face.

No doubt the Prince, despite his readiness to mow down everything in sight on a shoot, completely lost his nerve when he was unarmed – and left the gate open in his hasty retreat.

And Faro would have given much to know more about that quarrel between the Prince and his equerry, the reasons for which he had delicately omitted in his letter to the Queen. Had Poppy Elrigg been the reason, or had the Prince lost at cards?

Whatever the quarrel, it had been serious enough for

54

him to cut short his visit to Elrigg. Was his anxiety to escape scandal or blackmail the only reason why he had been reported as 'abroad' and unable to attend the funeral of his equerry?

But Faro now had another strand leading into the labyrinth.

Yarrow's revelations regarding Sir Archie's nephew who was also in the vicinity had posed yet another question over the events of that day.

As he made notes of his interviews with the local police, Faro was left with an uneasy feeling of something he had missed. Something of vital importance. And what began as a personal command from Her Majesty, to prove for her anxious pride that her son, the future King of England, was not a coward, was already showing unmistakable signs of developing into a worse scandal.

Murder.

As he walked briskly in the direction of the castle to talk again to the devoted couple who had been his prime suspects, Lady Elrigg and her stepson Mark, Faro was already adding one other name:

That of Mr Hector Elrigg.

Even as he did so, he realized his behaviour was one of habit. But it was also quite out of order and he must not give in to temptation but merely regard it as an exercise in detection to fill in the few days before Vince's arrival, an investigation dictated by personal curiosity and the challenge set by a long-buried victim, no clues and some very vague suspects.

If murder was involved then he had no rights beyond turning over any evidence he found to Sergeant Yarrow, who would doubtless stir himself out of the torpor of Elrigg village and its feudal system and, remembering his old skills, do an efficient job of seeing justice done.

As for himself, he must return to Edinburgh, report to Her Majesty that her son was guiltless – of cowardice.

She need never know that he had narrowly escaped being involved in a murder inquiry, much more difficult to live down for the future King of England than a divorce scandal.

Chapter 9

Later that morning, Faro was retracing his steps along the Castle drive. He was in no very good temper, for it had been a wasted journey. The ancient butler had informed him quite firmly that there was no one at home and, in terms that suggested shocked effrontery, no, he had not the least idea when Her Ladyship and Mr Mark might be expected to return.

The weather too fitted Faro's mood of exasperation. How on earth did one bring any possible criminal investigation to a satisfying conclusion in such circumstances as he faced at Elrigg? Small wonder policemen like Dewar and Yarrow were only too glad to accept 'accidental death' and close the inquiries as fast as possible.

Rounding up suspects over a wide area, much less trying to interview them, faced with ancient retainers like the Castle butler, was a daunting prospect for even the most experienced detective.

Police procedure in Edinburgh's Central Office, well documented and with carriages on hand, had never seemed more agreeable to Faro as he walked past the archery field, the scene of the Elriggs' medieval pursuits.

He quickened his steps as, on both sides of the drive, storm-tossed rhododendrons shivered and swayed in the rising wind. If those swift-gathering rain clouds broke, he reckoned he was in for a thorough soaking long before he reached the inn.

Seconds later, the warning patter of heavy raindrops on the trees above his head had him running towards the gate lodge. But the wooden porch he hoped would offer temporary shelter was already leaking badly.

As he leaned back against the door, it yielded to his touch. Presumably the cottage was not empty after all and, anxious not to alarm the occupants, he applied his hand to the brass knocker. When there was no response, he stepped inside.

A woman's voice from upstairs greeted his entrance.

'Go through to the kitchen. The back door won't close properly and the cupboard door has jammed. I'll be with you in a minute.'

Faro did as he was bid. The cottage obviously had not been lived in for some time. It felt damp and unwelcoming, the furniture stood shrouded in attitudes of neglect that he felt often characterized inanimate objects in deserted houses.

In the kitchen, a fire recently lit crackled feebly and a book lying open beside provisions scattered on the table suggested a new tenant had taken possession.

Insatiably curious about other people's reading matter, from which Faro believed there might be much to be gained in the matter of observation and deduction, he picked it up and read:

We hear every day of murders committed in the country. Brutal and treacherous murders; slow, protracted agonies from poisons administered by some kindred hand; sudden and violent deaths by cruel blows, inflicted with a stake cut from some spreading oak, whose every shadow promised – Peace. In the country of which I write, I have been shown a meadow in which, on a quiet summer Sunday evening, a young farmer murdered the girl who loved and trusted him; and yet, even now, with the stain of that foul deed upon it, the aspect of the spot is – Peace. No species of crime has ever been committed in the worst rookeries of the Seven Dials that has not been also done in the face of that rustic calm which still, in spite of all, we look on with a tender, half-mournful yearning, and associate with – Peace.

The passage was heavily underscored, the word 'Elrigg?' written in the margin. But what surprised Faro most of all was its title: *Lady Audley's Secret*. Written by Mary Elizabeth Braddon in the 1860s, it belonged to the category of 'Sensation' novels, whereby authors came by their plots from real-life murders and sensational crimes reported in the newspapers.

'Have you found the problem?' called the voice from upstairs, obviously wondering at his silence.

'I believe so,' Faro called and tackling the back door discovered the cause to be rusted hinges. Such a domestic challenge was always calculated to put him on his mettle as his housekeeper Mrs Brook was well aware.

On a shelf beside the kitchen dresser, he found what he was looking for, an oil can. A liberal application soon had the offending door working nicely again and, encouraged by this success, he was turning his attention to the cupboard door when light footsteps in the passage announced the occupier's approach.

'There are some other jobs you might tackle now that you've deigned to put in an appearance.'

Half turning his head in the gloom, with sinking heart Faro recognized the acid tones of the chilly lady who he had fondly imagined was now travelling far from Elrigg.

She was not a prepossessing sight, her abundant hair tied back loosely in a scarf and clad in a capacious and none too clean apron. She regarded him curiously.

'So, you are the new factor. Well, well,' she added as if surprised by the discovery. 'They said you might look in.'

Indignant, Faro stood up and drew himself to his full height. Unperturbed, she looked him over and taking in every detail of his appearance she said: 'Or am I mistaken? Is it the new gardener, you are?'

This was too much even for Faro. Notoriously uncaring in sartorial matters, he decided that although his clothes were by no means new, they did not merit such an outrageous assumption.

'No, madam,' he said coldly. 'I am neither gardener nor factor. I happened to be passing on my way from the Castle when the rain began – I was simply taking shelter—'

'Spying – ' she interrupted, pointing a finger at him.

'I beg your pardon?'

'Spying,' she repeated accusingly. 'Of course, you're a policeman.'

Taken aback, he stared at her. 'What makes you think—?'

'Oh, don't bother to deny it. I saw you going into the police station this morning. I guessed right, didn't I?' she demanded triumphantly. 'You're here about Sir Archie?'

Faro remained speechless as she continued: 'You'll get no help from Constable Dewar, I'm afraid. He's not very good at his job. Or that poor doomed fellow Yarrow, who's in charge—'

'What makes you say he's doomed?'

She looked at him strangely. 'I just know such things. I can see them written in people's faces.'

'Indeed. Psychic, are you?' he said mockingly.

She shrugged. 'Sometimes. I know things. I get flashes about people. Like you – like policemen,' she added sourly.

With the kitchen table between them, they glared at each other, adversaries poised in anticipation of the next move.

Finally, she gave way, and with a shrug walked over to the back door. Opening and closing it a few times, she nodded and said grudgingly:

'You did a good job, I'll say that for you. Thanks. I didn't feel very secure or very comfortable with it open to the four winds.'

'So you're a town lady?'

'Ye–es. How did—?'

'Country folk don't lock doors.'

60

'*Touché.*' For the first time she smiled, an expression, Faro admitted reluctantly, that quite transformed her face.

As he walked towards the front door, she said: 'What about the cupboard then?'

Faro looked at her and went over to the offending door. A vigorous tug and it responded. Turning, he gave her a grin of satisfaction. 'That's all it needed.'

'I see,' she said slowly. 'Brute strength! That was the answer.'

Faro merely nodded and preparing to take his leave, he asked: 'How long have you been living here?'

'Oh, about a month – on and off. I come and go.'

'You're not from these parts, are you?'

'Neither are you,' she said sharply.

Again Faro was taken aback, but before he could reply she said: 'I'm Irish. I took you for a Scot at first, but your accent isn't quite right.'

Faro smiled. 'That's very perceptive of you. I'm from Orkney.'

She opened the door. 'I've never been there.'

On the doorstep he turned. 'Are you staying here long?'

'Depends,' she said suspiciously.

Faro was about to ask 'On what?' As if reading his thoughts, she added: 'Depends on when my money runs out.' Poking her head out, she looked at the sky and dismissed him with the words: 'The rain's stopped. You can go now.'

As he stepped outside, she said: 'Name's Imogen Crowe.'

'Pleased to meet you, Miss Crowe,' he said, feeling hypocritical.

'How do you know I'm "Miss"?' she demanded.

'That's easy.' He pointed to her hand. 'No ring.'

And as he walked away, she called: 'What's your name?'

'Faro. Jeremy Faro.'

'Is that Sergeant or just plain Constable Faro?'

'Just plain Mister will do nicely. I'm an insurance

assessor,' he said acidly, in time to see a grin of mocking disbelief on her face as she banged the door behind him too quickly for politeness.

Going over that brief conversation, he didn't even give her credit for guessing he was a policeman, although that was extraordinary. He must take more care in future. There might be others about Elrigg as sharp as Miss Crowe, but he doubted that.

He didn't like her. He had no logical reason except hurt male pride and something about her that quite illogically nettled him. And almost angrily he shook his head, in an attempt to dismiss her completely from his thoughts.

At the inn a letter from Vince awaited him. 'Have managed to get an invitation to Miss Gilchrist's eightieth birthday celebration. Arriving with Owen and Olivia on Saturday. Plan to take an extra couple of days off, give Balfour a chance to become better acquainted with the patients! If you're not too busy with crime, I'd appreciate the opportunity of some decent tramping about, go to Hexham and walk the Roman Wall.'

Faro groaned. Vince never considered distances, while he became less agreeably aware that his feet, like his teeth, were not what they had been twenty-five years ago when the young lad from Orkney, Constable Jeremy Faro, had joined the Edinburgh City Police. To wear and tear of the damage done by years of ill-fitting boots, time had added sundry injuries acquired during many an alter-cation with villains.

Old stab and gun wounds to various parts of his body still plagued his extremely robust frame. Sore feet were more easily dealt with. He had found a temporary cure, and liked nothing better than pleasurably soaking them in a basin of warm soapy water which Mrs Brook sym-pathetically provided for him after supper. With a pipe of tobacco and a book propped before him, he was quite addicted to this secret vice. Such bliss – as he wriggled his toes, his joy was complete.

He preferred not to think of that other bane of his

life. Toothache. That too was becoming more frequent, although he was consoled by the dental surgeon on his good fortune in having all his front teeth, top and bottom, and most of his back molars in fine condition (the result of good heredity and rare indulgence in sweet things).

Vince found his attitude extraordinary. That a brave man who fearlessly faced death and injuries inflicted by violent criminals would suffer any agony rather than the inevitable extraction of an aching tooth. As for Faro, he seldom considered the miraculous human machine that carried him through day after relentless day, except when it threw out an occasional warning that chasing criminals had a definitely ageing effect.

Pride, however, forbade any dwelling at length on his personal weaknesses of foot and mouth to his young stepson. After all, a man in his early forties wasn't all that old. There were politicians and a monarch ruling the country who were much older than himself, not to mention policemen still walking the beat. Men like Constable Dewar.

Over a pint of ale and a game pie in the almost deserted dining room of the inn, Faro returned to Sir Archie's fatal accident – or was it murder? Glancing over the notes of his interview with Lady Elrigg and Mark, he had reached certain conclusions which might be significant.

Dewar had been helpful in filling in some of the background details and Faro was now almost certain that no wounded bull had been involved and that horns, stolen earlier from the inn's public bar, were the murder weapon, inflicting the fatal wound to lead the doctor and the two local policeman away from the truth, that Sir Archie had met his death at the hands of some person or persons as yet unknown.

He decided that a talk to the village doctor was his next step but, perhaps of greater importance, a visit to the angry young nephew Hector whose excavations of the hillfort were within sight of the copse where his uncle had died.

In weather unreliable from hour to hour, vacillating

from warm sunshine to driving rain, he set forth from the inn wrapped about temporarily in the splendour of an afternoon when the world held its breath.

Here was a day that had never heard of grey skies, of storms and cruel winds as it basked in the dazzling greens and innocent white blossom of a May morning. A lark blissfully hurled its triumphant song into a sky of celestial blue as he quickened his steps up the road.

To reach the hillfort he had to cross a strip of open pasture, domain of the wild cattle, and, leaving the road, he opened the gate cautiously, breathing freely again when he saw they were far up the hill. But even at that distance he felt naked and vulnerable, for they ceased grazing and fixed their eyes on him, all heads suddenly turned in his direction, as if they were well aware of his unease.

Hurrying towards the hillfort, he realized this was another wasted journey. There was no sign of Hector Elrigg, although his absence provided a chance to inspect the excavations more closely. He was not sure what he hoped to find, but it offered no helpful clues to the solution of the mystery.

Changing direction, he walked rapidly to the shelter of the trees across the deserted field, where he again examined the spot where Dewar had found Elrigg. Apart from a few broken branches the ground had healed and there was nothing to connect murder with that fatal misadventure.

Enjoying the warm sunshine on his back, he sat down on a large stone to enjoy a pipe. The crumbling wall beside him was part of a winter pen to give the sheep shelter. Looking round idly, he noticed what appeared to be the tip of a broken branch sticking out between the stones.

A sharp tug released it from its anchor. No branch emerged but the single stiletto-sharp horn of a bull. He gazed at it triumphantly. He had not the slightest doubt that what he held was once part of the pair stolen from the inn.

The murder weapon.

He examined it more closely: the ominous dark stain on the tip could be dried blood. Deciding this evidence might be useful and not wishing to be seen with it in his possession, he tucked it up his jacket sleeve for a closer inspection later.

Emerging from the copse, his back was now turned towards the cattle but the trees concealed him from their gaze. He was not consoled for although there were no animals visible except for a few grazing sheep, his mind dwelt nervously on fences and open gates.

Not only the king bull was dangerous, he realized, but a young and skittish male, moving apart from the herd and for reasons of its own, of a possibly homicidal disposition, could be equally damaging when on the rampage.

He walked quickly in the direction of the road and, conscious of the lack of any shelter, glanced back frequently over his shoulder. Alert at every sound, he found himself reliving that moment in his childhood near his aunt's Deeside croft more than thirty years ago.

How terrifyingly the ground had shaken under his feet at the thunderous charge, the snort of rage as the great red shaggy beast hurtled towards him through the mist.

He knew how narrowly he had escaped death that morning and, for years afterwards, he had awakened screaming with the smell of the enraged Highland bull's hot breath on his neck, its murderous sharp horns at his heels . . .

Shuddering from remembrance, he was within sight of the gate leading to the road when the chill gathering about his shoulders was not from fear but from a black sky replacing what had been cloudless sunshine minutes ago.

The next moment the cloud burst overhead and hailstones pelted down on him. He began to run . . .

Thunder rattled across the sky, shaking the hills and, almost within safety and the fenced road, he heard the ground echoing with the monstrous sound of hoofs . . .

Chapter 10

The beast pounding towards Faro along the road was no wild bull, merely a rather stout horse and trap bearing an elderly gentleman sheltering under a large umbrella.

'Whoa!' And, stopping alongside, he leaned out. 'Care for a lift?'

'I would be most grateful.'

As Faro climbed in, the man who was clad in a handsome tweed greatcoat handed him a waterproof cape. 'Keep the worst of the rain off you, although I dare say it'll pass over in a minute.'

Even as he spoke, the sun came out again, scudding across the field, and the angry clouds were swept away, their rain sheets now lying heavily to the east.

'That's that,' said the man, closing the umbrella. 'I'm Dr Brand, by the way.'

An unexpected stroke of luck, Faro thought, as the doctor continued: 'Saw you crossing the field. Out walking were you?' Acquainted with everyone in the village, he was obviously curious about this stranger and it was in Faro's own interest to enlighten him.

'Oh, I see. An insurance assessor. Of course,' the doctor nodded sympathetically, 'the family can take no chances.'

'I suppose you examined Sir Archie,' said Faro tentatively.

'I did indeed. Nothing I could do by that time. Clearly an accident. Gored by one of the cattle. Such things do happen. We do have the very occasional accident,' he added apologetically.

'I remember reading something about an earlier incident in the newspapers,' said Faro encouragingly. 'A young fellow staying at the castle, was it not?'

The doctor nodded. 'An actor. Philip Gray, you may have seen him on the stage in Edinburgh. I only heard his Shakespearean monologues one evening at the Castle. But I was most impressed.'

'You attended him when he was injured?'

'I examined his body, if that's what you mean,' said the doctor grimly. 'Death by misadventure. His horse had thrown him, he had a fractured skull. Of course, he had no right to be in the grazing pastures at all. Guests are always warned that the cattle are dangerous.'

'But he had ignored the warning?'

The doctor sighed. 'I understood that the, er, guest he was out riding with had dared him to venture out and bring back the horns from a beast the shooting party had wounded earlier that week.'

'Not a very sensible thing to do from all accounts,' Faro volunteered.

'As he soon found out,' said the doctor grimly. 'You know what these young fellows are like, must prove themselves. Sense of honour and all that nonsense. The beast wasn't too badly wounded to charge him and gore him to death.' He shook his head. 'It's this damned archaic system to blame. Sportsmen they call themselves. Rounding up the beasts and choosing their target. All of them having a go at it with their arrows first. Shouldn't be allowed. One man, one bullet – that's the humane way.'

He paused and sighed. 'The poor lad made it to the copse over there, same place where they found Elrigg.'

'An odd coincidence?'

Dr Brand ignored his interruption. 'Elrigg might have survived, he had severe but not fatal neck and head injuries sustained in the fall and was probably unconscious.'

He paused like a man who had a lot more to say on that subject but had remembered in time that his passenger was a stranger. He shrugged. 'Perhaps he never regained consciousness when the cow got him. One can only hope so, anyway.'

'Cow? I thought only the bulls were dangerous.'

The doctor smiled. 'The cow is just as dangerous if she has just dropped a calf. This is the time of year and they often choose a sheltered place, away from the herd. Like the copse. There'd been a stalking party out from the castle the day before the accident, it was deer and birds they were interested in but that would make a cow very nervous.

'That's my theory, anyway. These animals have their own laws, far older and wiser than man's. I was brought up on a farm. We were used to taking in newborn orphaned animals and raising them by hand. Tried it once when I first came here. Found this newborn calf, abandoned or orphaned, I thought. It was getting dark, a freezing cold night, so I wrapped it in a blanket hoping to keep it alive till next day when I'd see if its mother had come back for it.'

He paused and sighed deeply. 'I was young and idealistic then, couldn't bear the thought of an animal suffering. I soon learned my lesson,' he added harshly.

'Did she charge you too?'

'No. But when I went back the next day to see how the wee creature was,' he shuddered, 'there was nothing left of it but a few bones and bits of skin. But the hoofmarks were visible where it had lain. Looked as if there had been a stampede and it had been trampled into the earth. Their sense of smell is acute and if a calf is handled by a human the other animals detect the smell and kill it.'

'But surely—'

'I know what you're going to say, but you're quite wrong. I had made the crucial mistake of humans interfering with wild creatures. I had mismanaged my rescue attempt and turned the calf into an alien from the herd. They had their own ways of dealing with that,' he added grimly.

'Make no mistake about these animals. They are quite

unique, they have a society evolved through hundreds – perhaps thousands of years. The herd is under complete control of one beast. Only the fittest and strongest in the herd ever becomes king bull. And during the two or three years until he is successfully challenged and defeated in combat by a younger rival, he reigns supreme and sires all the calves that are born.'

As he talked, he let the reins go slack and the horse, finding this an agreeable change of pace, ambled slowly along.

'I've been fascinated by their behaviour for years. I've watched them, through a telescope – from my house over there,' he added pointing to the east of the village. 'Once I saw a young bull come out of the herd, it was the bellowing that drew me. I saw him pawing the ground, the old bull doing likewise. They charged – and this time it was a fight to the death.'

'You say they've been here for thousands of years – where did they come from?'

'No one can answer that. Bones which might belong to them have been found in the hillfort, so they provided meat for prehistoric man. At one time they were thought to be related to the Highland cattle, a sort of albino relative. But that has been disproved.'

'How have they managed to survive without inbreeding with other domestic cattle?'

'Because they've never been domestic. It's possible that being white they were regarded as sacred – kept for some ancient religious ritual. They've never been known to throw a coloured or even partly coloured calf. As for their survival, who knows? It is against all the odds since the cows are poor breeders, suckle their calves for long periods. Nature's way of preventing the herd increasing rapidly.'

'I'm surprised that they survived the moss troopers and the Border reivers. I understood they carried off everything they could lay hands on.'

Dr Brand laughed. 'Aye, what they laid hands on, right

enough. But there was no hope of laying hands on these beasts and driving them back across the border. Much too wild and fierce to be treated like the ordinary domestic variety.'

Turning, he looked back towards the hill. 'I'd advise you to take great care about walking across these fields. I was quite alarmed when I saw you. Someone should have warned you. Where are you staying?' When Faro told him, he nodded. 'I shall have a severe word with him, have a notice posted in very large letters.'

Pausing, he regarded Faro sharply. 'I don't think you are taking me seriously, sir.'

'I am, doctor, I am indeed.'

'Make no mistake about it. These animals are extremely dangerous. And they have perception beyond what we humans can understand.' Shading his eyes, the doctor pointed with his whip. 'I don't suppose you've been here long enough to observe that they never take their eyes off any humans in the vicinity. We are under constant surveillance. There is always one animal watching, on guard, somewhere,' he added with an uneasy laugh.

'So you think there might have been a calf in the vicinity that Sir Archie didn't know about.'

'It certainly wasn't a wounded king bull, anyway. Saw him large as life grazing with the herd the next day. Besides the horns – the goring injury, I mean – they hadn't penetrated deep enough for a really angry charging bull. Makes a nasty mess, I can tell you. But this was just one hole, quite neat, just an inch or two deep.'

'Is that so?' said Faro thoughtfully. According to Constable Dewar there had been no hoofmarks of a charging animal either. 'You had no doubts about the cause of death when you signed the death certificate?'

'None at all. The coroner's inquest was a mere waste of time. Death by misadventure, there couldn't be any other verdict in the circumstances. I'll let you have his report if you need it for your firm. And if you're interested in the cattle, there's some old documents in the Castle library,

I'm sure Lady Elrigg would let you see them . . .'

The road narrowed steeply and they were passing by the tiny Saxon church with its graveyard, deep in primroses and wood anemones. A blackbird sang on one of the tombstones, the feathers on its throat fluttering, its piercing sweetness a eulogy to an awakening world.

Faro sighed. 'Gives you hope, doesn't it? I wouldn't mind lying here to all eternity with a requiem like that every spring.'

At his side the doctor had raised his top hat to reveal a mane of silver hair and lapsed into a reverent silence. 'Spring's a sad time for some people, for the ones who are left.'

'I understand, sir, only too well.' Noting the doctor's grief-stricken expression, Faro remembered that his Lizzie had died with their newborn son beside her on a June morning eight years ago. 'To lose one's partner in life . . .' He paused. 'Your wife, sir?' he said gently.

'Lost her long ago,' was the bitter response. 'God only knows what sky her bones lie under. It was my daughter I lost. My dearest only child.' His voice broke and, geeing up the pony, he drove fast into the village, his lips a tight line of misery, while at his side Faro cursed his own lack of tact.

Setting him down at the inn, Dr Brand spoke again. 'You must forgive my outburst, sir, to you a stranger, quite unforgivable.'

'It is I who must apologize, sir. But I do know something of the loss you have suffered. A child dying—'

'Dying. She didn't die. She should have been alive today, she was seventeen with all the world before her. She didn't die. She was murdered.'

At Faro's shocked expression, he jabbed a finger in the direction of the Castle. 'And they killed her.'

Chapter 11

As Faro entered the inn, Bowden ceased his polishing of the counter long enough to say: 'Duffy has been in looking for you, Mr Faro.'

'Are you sure it was me?'

'You're the insurance mannie, aren't you?'

'Did he say what he wanted?'

'Not my business to ask, sir. But knowing Duffy I'd say there was money involved. Wouldn't you, gentlemen?'

Bowden grinned at Yarrow and Dewar. About to depart, they paused long enough to give Faro a decidedly searching glance. It suggested that they also suspected he might be involved in some of the poacher's dubious activities.

'He said he'll see you when he comes in for his pint of ale later on,' said Bowden as Faro made his way towards his room.

What could the poacher want with him? Faro was curious and hopeful too. From his vast experience of the criminal world he did not doubt that this new turn of events indicated information was for sale.

Beyond his window was a pageant of undulating hills, cloudless skies. Trees moved in slow ecstasy to their burden of soft breeze and birdsong, a scene characteristic of any gentle sleepy village that one could hardly credit with violence. Even the ivy-clad walls of its ancient cottages seemed to have grown naturally out of the tranquil earth rather than the stones hewed by men.

A traveller passing through *en route* for Scotland would think nothing ever happened here, that time had passed it by, but Faro was aware of the elements of passion that lurked behind such quiet exteriors and that this was a more elemental world than the one he had left a short time ago in Edinburgh. With total recall he saw again the words written by Mary Elizabeth Braddon:

> We hear every day of murders committed in the country . . . No species of crime has ever been committed in the worst rookeries of the Seven Dials that has not been also done in the face of that rustic calm . . .

Words that Imogen Crowe had heavily underscored. She had written 'Elrigg?' beside them. Why?

Do not be fooled, Jeremy Faro, he told himself as he considered his evidence so far.

Philip Gray had been riding with the Prince. They had quarrelled when the Prince accused him of cheating at cards. Bertie had returned alone. Later, when the actor's horse came in riderless, a search party found him gored to death.

Sir Archie had met his death in suspiciously similar circumstances. Two men dying in identical place and manner, months apart, after quarrels with the same illustrious guest, hinted not merely at coincidence, but at murder.

If only the trail was still warm. Any clues regarding Gray's death by misadventure had vanished beneath last year's fallen autumn leaves and for the last four weeks Sir Archie had rested in his grave.

The Prince had been the last to see both men alive and Faro remembered grimly the letter Her Majesty had shown him.

He wished he had been allowed to make a copy of it for a more careful study of the schoolboy pleading: 'Don't blame me. It wasn't my fault, Mama.'

73

Her son's innocence was all he had to prove. Murder in this case was not his business.

If only he could leave it at that . . .

From the valise under his bed, Faro withdrew the bull's horn. Weighing it in his hands, he knew how Sir Archie had been murdered. Almost as if he had been present, a silent witness, he could conjure up the exact picture of Elrigg's last moments.

The horn had been broken off from the pair stolen from the public bar downstairs.

Archery was the local sport and it would not have needed an expert marksman to realize that although it could not be fired with any accuracy from a crossbow, it presented a splendid potential as a murder weapon. By a piece of good fortune his opportunity came when he found his victim semi-conscious and unable to rise from the ground.

Faro frowned. That posed a question. It had to be someone who was in the area at the time and witnessed the accident. It might have been that Sir Archie was still alive when the first of the rescue party arrived, perhaps one of the tenants alerted by Constable Dewar on his way through the village. For a man with a grievance, a unique opportunity of settling an old score.

Once the deed was done, the murderer withdrew the horn and thrust it into the wall, where with luck he hoped it would never be noticed.

With circumstances of Philip Gray's death still fresh in everyone's mind, the possibility of foul play had never occurred. Neither Yarrow nor Dewar had thought to search the copse for evidence, indeed the constable's observation regarding the lack of hoofmarks had been mockingly dismissed.

Faro regarded the bull's horn thoughtfully. The question now was who had reached Sir Archie ahead of Yarrow and Dr Brand.

The only person he could safely eliminate was Lady Elrigg who had remained at the Castle. In a state of shock as befitted the newly widowed.

74

He knew nothing of any relationship with the young actor but he recalled vividly his first sight of Lady Elrigg and Mark leaving the archery field together. Had there been a sinister quality to their careless laughter?

Although Elrigg would be Mark's some day, did he see himself as a young knight ready to dare all – even murder – for the stepmother who could never be his wife?

Guilty lovers invariably provided the best motive for murder. From Biblical times to the present day that had been the case and Faro did not doubt it would continue until the final curtain descended on mankind. The male rivalry between the old and young was not unique. Just a mile away, that instinct for survival of the species was strong enough to drive young bulls to challenge the king for supremacy of the wild cattle herd.

The question was, did Lady Elrigg respond to Mark? If so, then she had the perfect reason for wishing to be rid of an elderly husband whose charm was limited to his bank account, especially when there was a fortune and a handsome, young and virile man to inherit. If Poppy Lynne had married Elrigg only for his fortune and with his stepson conspired in his murder, then Faro would feel no sympathy for either of them.

Was she morally responsible for Gray's death too, enticing men to kill for her love? The more facts Faro unearthed, the less he liked the unpleasant picture that his imagination created. One did not have to dig too deeply below the surface to discover that Elrigg was a man who made many enemies. Known as well as unknown – as yet!

Of the known enemies, Hector Elrigg had the best reason of all. Over the years, a festering rage and resentment that he was morally the rightful heir. He also had the best vantage point for murder, witnessing the accident from the hillfort, seeing the Prince ride off and finding his hated uncle helpless, had he seized the chance for revenge?

With the bull's horn?

Faro shook his head. No, it wouldn't do. Hector might have stolen the horns, but it was unlikely he could have secreted them away for just such a possibility. If they had been taken from the inn with such a plot in mind, then Sir Archie would have been lured to his death.

And it seemed highly unlikely that the future King of England could have dreamed up anything as subtle as the method used of diverting attention from his equerry's murder. Unless he had been the willing accomplice of Lady Elrigg. Would such a theory fit the Prince's panic-stricken retreat from the copse and his speedy departure from the Castle?

Faro doubted that. Bertie's constant fear of blackmail and his ready supply of mistresses made Poppy Elrigg in no way special or permanent. Merely one more dalliance, that was all.

Dismissing the Prince's role in his equerry's murder, Faro realized that anyone besides the poacher Duffy might have stolen the horns, hidden them away in the copse where they had been accidentally found by some-one from the village with murder in mind, that local tenant with reason to hate the laird.

Someone like Dr Brand who blamed his daughter's death on the Elriggs. (What had happened? Constable Dewar would no doubt reveal the circumstances if asked.)

Recalling the earlier part of his conversation with the doctor, all Faro now knew for certain was that Elrigg had been unconscious but not fatally injured when the Prince – and his horse – bolted.

And that brought him sharply back to the reason for his presence at Elrigg. His main purpose was to obey the Royal Command and report back to Her Majesty that the Prince of Wales was innocent of cowardice. This he could do with confidence, for if the hidden bull's horn was the weapon used to end Sir Archie's life, then it was unlikely indeed that the Prince had been the murderer.

But instead of being satisfied that he had completed his mission and returning to Edinburgh, he realized he was following the habit of a lifetime of police investigation and allowing himself to be drawn into a mystery that it was not

76

even his right to solve. That if the entire population of Elrigg decided to kill each other off, or their laird, this was the business of the Northumberland Constabulary to assist Sergeant Yarrow and Constable Dewar by the appointment of a detective experienced in murder investigations.

The evidence of his own eyes was, apart from finding the probable murder weapon, only circumstantial. But he wished he could have known the exact location of the possible suspects at the time of Sir Archie's death.

Replacing the horn reluctantly, as if by holding it in his hands he might extract by supernatural means the identity of the murderer, he made a mental note to be firm with himself and concentrate on the history of Elrigg while he awaited Vince's arrival, meanwhile ignoring any grisly secrets of the past that were none of his business.

He would begin by having another look at the hillfort.

Chapter 12

Hector Elrigg's greeting was cordial. In more leisurely circumstances than their first encounter in the police station, Faro saw that generations of Elrigg warriors had created the young man's strong physique and vital personality. A fighting man in the tradition of Harry Hotspur. Leaning on his spade, Hector said: 'Good day to you, sir. Interested in our old hillfort, are you?'

Faro murmured that he was and Hector nodded eagerly. Tapping the ground with his foot, he said: 'You're standing on the oldest part of Elrigg, it's been here since the dawn of history, when this entire area was covered with a vast forest and the inhabitants had just left their nomadic ways and decided to make places of settlement where they could trade, chat, make marriage contracts, worship – become a community.'

'Does your hillfort predate the wild cattle?'

Hector shook his head. 'Who can tell? Certainly the ancestors of our cattle would have provided meat for their spears. Come, walk round with me.'

As Faro followed him across the grassy mound, which was the size of a small field, only piles of stones and a few broken walls marked the spot that Hector told him lay within a circle of byroads.

'Once it rose to about five hundred feet, crowned with a camp for whoever made himself chief. Even in those days, there were men who had more physical strength, cunning and insight to come out on top as leaders.'

As they climbed up the slope, Hector said, 'Look back.

This is a good time to be here, when the sun is sinking. See how it lights up the contours. Those parallel lines you see under the turf are cultivation terraces.'

And walking quickly ahead, he jumped on a large boulder and pointed back the way they had come.

'Those humps in the ground are the remains of hut circles, folds for cattle, and burial cairns.'

'Have you found anything interesting?'

'A few urn burials, amber necklaces, silver rings, and so forth.' He smiled. 'A liking for luxury and personal vanity is not news, the powerful and rich had jewellery and other ornaments, superior pottery and weapons. Power takes many forms but the display of one's riches was necessary and popular then as a fine house, a carriage and horses, is today. The secret of power for early man was their ability to use the landscape not only to survive but to produce a surplus that they could use to bargain and trade with, to buy slaves and most important to buy allegiance from chiefs to serve them.

'Of course, like everyone then and now, they mislaid and lost things, broke them or threw them away. Except that, as they didn't have much to lose, they left us enough to give us some idea of their lives. Their technology depended largely on flint – flint that could be smashed up, flaked and worked into tools of every variety – blades, scrapers and arrowheads. With the discovery of flint animals could be killed, eaten and their hides used for clothes, tents, waterbags.'

Hector paused and pointed to the skyline. 'You get the best view from the top of the hill yonder, worth the climb. The headless women. If you aren't afraid to go there.'

'The cattle, you mean.'

'No. Even the cattle are scared of them.'

'Really.'

'It's the noise they make that scares them off. The presence of the old gods.'

Faro smiled.

'An unbeliever, eh. Well, take it from me, whatever you

want to call that primeval force, it's worthy of respect. And fear. It can be very unnerving if you're up there in a rising wind. First it sounds as if the stones are sighing, then crying – that's when you want to run . . .'

'Has anyone tried to find the cause?'

'Oh, I know the cause,' said Hector cheerfully. 'Natural erosion has resulted in fluting and gulleys on the stones. The wind rushes through them rather like organ pipes. That's the scientific explanation, but try to persuade generations of the ignorant and superstitious that they are not the cries of Celtic princesses turned to stone. And when they scream then disaster will strike Elrigg.'

'Have you ever excavated the site?'

Hector's face darkened. 'I've tried to. I'm certain there is evidence to link the date of the stones with the hillfort, perhaps they were part of a religious ceremonial or the burial site of some important tribal chief. But I've been denied that right.'

He paused and regarded Faro suspiciously for the first time. 'Wait a moment. I have seen you before. At the police station.'

'That is so.'

When Faro did not offer any further explanation, Hector continued: 'Are you here to register for the archery contest?'

'Alas, no.'

'A pity. You have the look of a man who might be handy with weapons,' he said, surveying him candidly.

But Faro refused to be drawn.

Hector continued to regard him curiously. 'You seem remarkably well informed, sir. What exactly brings you to these parts?'

'Insurance business, alas.' Faro tried to sound casual. 'All rather boring, I'm afraid.'

'Connected with my late uncle, I presume.'

'Yes.'

'He was a bastard and he deserved to die. A few acres of his precious ground, a chance to discover the secret of the stones. That's all I've ever wanted, all I ever asked him for. He owed me a lot more than that – a damned lot more.'

He stopped, shrugged. 'I won't bore you with the details. It's a very long and sordid story. All I can tell you is that they're a rum lot up at the Castle.'

'In what way?'

Hector stared at the horizon. 'Oh, you know. The young and beautiful actress who marries an old man for his money. Brings one of her London actress friends with her as companion. Can't blame her insisting on that as part of the deal. Life would be pretty intolerable for her otherwise. But her friend, Miss Kent, I don't know how she sticks it. A far cry from the stage. Poppy must have made it worth her while – Miss Kent was never a great beauty with all the world and the Prince of Wales at her feet.'

He looked at Faro as he said it. So he knew the identity of the visitor at the time of Sir Archie's fatal accident. And as Faro listened and watched Hector's expression change to one of wistfulness, he realized that the nephew might also have a motive of jealousy, mesmerized by Poppy Elrigg too although he might qualify only for one of 'all the world'.

'It would have made more sense for Mark to fall for the companion, wouldn't it?' Hector went on. 'But no, it's the stepma he wants. Miss Kent would have been much safer.'

'How safer?'

Hector laughed and, ignoring the question, he said: 'I've nothing against young Mark. Like the boy, I must say. We've always got along splendidly. I even gave him his first archery lessons. He saw me as a kind of latterday Robin Hood. Used to come and watch me dig when he came home from boarding school. He was intrigued by the possibilities of old graves and skeletons, the usual schoolboy preoccupation with buried treasure and that nonsense. I gave him a spade and a bit of encouragement.'

He smiled at the remembrance before adding: 'He

didn't like his stepfather even then and their relationship didn't improve with time. Poppy's arrival was probably the last straw—'

And Faro wondered how much Mark's young life had been influenced by Hector's grudge against Sir Archie. He could well imagine the impressionable schoolboy with a case of hero worship for this romantic relative who searched ancient ruins for buried treasure.

Hector was eyeing him candidly. 'Insurance investigator, you say?' Without waiting for Faro's reply, he continued, 'If you'd been a policeman, I'd have said there are one or two who'll be mightily pleased that Uncle Archie got his just deserts. He killed a beater once. Drunk he was, should not have been in charge of a loaded shotgun. An accident, everyone covered up like mad. Young lad about twelve.'

'From these parts?'

'No. From Durham somewhere. He was staying with relations, farmers over Flodden way. Can't remember the details, illness in the family, something of the sort. An only child. Went to school here for a while and got on well with young Mark, the two of them used to come to the dig. His aunt and uncle were so upset by the tragedy they couldn't settle afterwards and moved away. Felt guilty, although it was none of their fault, poor souls.

'And then there's Dr Brand, his daughter drowned herself, suicide. Plenty would say she was driven to it.'

Faro recalled the doctor's words as Hector went on.

'She was a bright, clever girl, working for the summer on cataloguing family documents for my uncle. She left in a hurry. Rumour had it that she was pregnant – and the whispers were that it was Uncle Archie's bairn. Later it came out that the factor had been dallying with her. He'd been sacked for embezzlement, bolted for London before he could be arrested, leaving her in the lurch.'

He sighed. 'She walked into the ornamental lake by the walled garden. My uncle showed some finer feelings – or some remorse, by having the lake drained.'

82

'So all this will go to Mark now?'

Hector did not seem perturbed. 'That is so, since there is no issue, legitimate or otherwise. Mark's mother was ten years older than my uncle, plain but very wealthy. Nice woman, kind too. Coal owner's widow. There were no children. He was out of luck with Poppy too. Five years and no sign of an heir.'

A childless marriage, a barren wife. How often Faro had heard that. The bane of rich men and noble lairds with much to leave and desperate for a son to leave it to. Kings had murdered their queens and lords abandoned their ladies for just such a reason. In the new society even rich merchants keen to establish a dynasty had been known to be crafty and merciless in ridding themselves of a barren wife.

It remained one of the best of all possible motives for murder. If Poppy had been the victim instead of her husband.

Hector squinted up at the sky. 'We'll have rain soon. Must get on with things, unless you'd like a shot with a spade too.' And nodding towards a cottage half hidden by trees, 'I live over there. If you change your mind and feel like some healthy exercise any time.'

'I'll bear it in mind.' Faro pointed to the standing stones outlined against the sky. 'Meanwhile I think I'll brave the headless women.'

Hector grinned. 'Walk round the field unless you want an encounter with the farmer – an earful of his bellowing could be more scaring than our stone ladies' vocal qualities.'

Faro smiled. 'Constable Dewar warned me.'

Hector regarded him coolly. 'You don't look to me like a man who scares easily. What was it you said you were – an insurance assessor?'

And his accompanying laugh, with its note of disbelief, reminded Faro sharply how thin his disguise was.

As he climbed the steep hill, the sun beat down straight

into his eyes. The stones seemed to shiver in the glowing transparent light. Occasionally he stopped and shaded his eyes. Once or twice he could have sworn he saw a dark shadow move swiftly across his line of vision.

At last, following the rough path, he reached the perimeter of the circle. His mind far away, he almost leaped from his skin when a woman's face stared down at him.

Not stone, but flesh and blood with dark red hair and green eyes. A face as cold as the stones, whose response to his friendly greeting was to gather up her papers, tuck them swiftly into her valise and jump down the other side of the circle.

'Wait,' he called. 'I didn't mean to intrude. Don't let me disturb you.'

Whether she heard him or not, he couldn't tell, his efforts rewarded by her fleeing back, her hair flowing out like a burning bush behind her as she leaped down through the stony field.

Obviously she feared an irate farmer less than himself, Faro thought. And watching her swift progress, half amused, half exasperated, he realized he had almost forgotten Imogen Crowe's existence.

About to retrace his steps, he noticed a slim book lying face downward where she had been sitting.

Glancing at the title, *The History of Civilization*, he thrust it into his pocket, only mildly curious about this dramatic change in reading matter or what interesting mission his arrival had interrupted to cause her precipitate flight.

He would hand in the book to the lodge sometime. A nuisance, and her own fault if she lost it. He had turned his attention to the stones when he heard a cry.

A human cry . . .

Chapter 13

The cry had issued not from the headless women behind him, but from the stony field.

Faro stared down from the perimeter of the circle. Imogen Crowe was lying on the ground about thirty yards away. She looked up, saw him and called: 'Help me, will you, please.'

What an irresistible invitation, he thought grimly and made his way carefully down the rough ground of the field.

'Are you hurt?' he asked, bending over her.

She struggled to sit up. 'Of course I'm hurt. I wouldn't call for help otherwise. My ankle, I think I've broken my bloody ankle. No, don't you touch it. Don't dare—'

And thrusting his hand away she seized her ankle between her hands and began to rub it vigorously, moaning a little as she did so. 'I twisted it on that bracken root. I just shot forward – and here I am.'

Faro stared down at her. 'You should have come up by the path at the edge of the field.'

'I did that.'

'Then why on earth didn't you go back the same way? Racing down the field like that . . .'

She shrugged and chose not to answer what was perfectly obvious and equally embarrassing: her eagerness to escape from him.

With a sigh, Faro looked down at her, held out his hands, still waiting to be thanked for his assistance: 'Can you stand?' he asked gently.

She stood up, wavered and with a cry would have fallen again but for Faro. She looked indignantly at his steadying hand on her arm as if she'd like to brush it off, given half a chance and a more reliable balance.

If only her damned ankle wasn't so sore. Now she had to rely on this wretched man. Nodding towards the still distant road, she said, 'Help me down there, will you.'

'Of course.' And bending over he picked her up bodily.

'What do you think you're doing?' she demanded angrily.

'Isn't that rather obvious, seeing that you are incapable of walking?'

'Put me down – at once.'

'As you wish,' Faro said coldly, setting her down so unceremoniously that she moaned, clutching her ankle as she tried to regain her balance.

'I – I can't.'

'Then will you allow me to assist you?' She put her arms around his neck and struggled no more as he carried her once more towards the stone circle.

'This isn't the way to the road.'

'I'm quite aware of that. But this is the way we are going. The way we both came up. Unless you want us both to have twisted ankles – or worse. A broken neck might be the answer . . .'

She struggled in his arms. 'This is nonsense. Put me down. I'll manage.'

Faro stopped, and again set her on her feet. 'Listen to me. Either you do as I say or I will leave you to make your own damned way back to Elrigg. I don't care either way.'

She was silent, staring at the ground.

'Agreed?'

She nodded and, with a sigh, he said: 'Off we go then.'

Lifting her more carefully this time he clambered up the last few yards very carefully. The terrain was strewn with smaller stones, boulders from the circle that had been eroded through the ages, washed by wind and weather down the field and were now barely but dangerously concealed by thick coarse grass.

'You shouldn't have taken it at a run. You could have hurt more than your ankle. Foolish creature.'

This expression was mild compared to what he wanted to say – and do – at that moment. She was behaving like a spoilt child and deserved more than a gentle reprimand. He pursed his lips grimly.

However, she was lighter than he had expected, small boned although she was quite tall. Bodily contact was not unpleasant, she was warm, sweet smelling, her hair resting against his cheek . . .

Damned woman. Damned woman, he muttered to himself and set her down rather more sharply than was kind on one of the flat stones within the circle. There, without a word of thanks, she began to moan and rub her injured ankle.

He pushed her hands aside. 'Let me look at it.'

Angrily she thrust him away. 'No. Leave me alone. There's nothing you can do. Unless you're a doctor.' And wriggling her foot, she winced. 'It's probably just sprained a little. If I could rest for a few minutes.'

'Very well,' he said wearily. 'Let me know when you're ready to go down.'

She looked towards the road, distant beyond the stony field. 'How can I walk that far?'

He looked at her. 'I'll see if I can find a stick somewhere. You can use that. If not, I'll carry you. You're not very heavy.'

She darted him an angry glance. As if the whole episode was his fault.

Never had he met such a thankless, ungracious young woman and he walked quickly away before she could think of any ill-natured comment.

Leaving her with little hope of finding a branch for support, he was glad to escape from her and to concentrate on his reason for coming here in the first place. The view was breathtaking. The site commanded a magnificent landscape over the Cheviots, reaching out to touch the border with Scotland.

As for the five headless women, they were less forbidding at close quarters than seen from below. On closer examination the torso shapes were the result of natural erosion, confirming Hector Elrigg's theory that the fluting effect might well produce alarming sounds when the wind was in the right direction.

He made his way carefully through the nettles, which were their natural protective vegetation and whose roots had long ago hidden any significant detail of what had been the purpose of their original builders.

Lost in thought, he was suddenly aware of Miss Crowe looking over his shoulder.

'You've been such a long time, I thought you'd gone without me,' she said anxiously, sounding so contrite and scared that, smiling kindly, he was able to bite back the words: As you richly deserved.

In no hurry to leave, he continued to look at the view, fascinated by the mystery of this strange prehistoric site.

As if reading his thoughts she said, 'Why were they put here?' – her voice a whisper as if they might be overheard, their presence resented by the ghosts of this ancient place. 'Do you have any idea? I mean, how were they carried up this steep hill?'

'They are questions to which we will never have proper answers, I'm afraid. No more than how the Pyramids of Egypt were built.'

Pointing towards a horizon where Scotland began: 'Defence? Was that what they had in mind?' she asked.

'Probably. A lookout post for the hillfort below.'

'It must have been more than that, surely. A lookout post wouldn't have lasted for thousands of years.' Caressing the outline of the nearest stone, she smiled. 'Could they have been Celtic princesses perhaps?'

Faro smiled. 'If you mean, is that winsome legend true, I can assure you of one thing. These stones had been well established for centuries, a landmark long before the Romans came.'

'Or before history was written.' She moved away from

the stone, hobbling a little. 'I think I will be able to manage now – if I may take your arm.'

'Of course.' He helped her from the perimeter of the stones to the edge of the field. 'What brought you here?'

'Oh, I don't know. Natural curiosity. It's an intriguing story, one wants to believe that it's true. At least I'd like to. And I wanted to know why the village people were so afraid, why they avoid it.'

Leaning against the fence for support, she pointed towards the Eildon hills. 'Have you read Sir Walter Scott, by any chance?'

'Of course,' Faro replied. 'He is one of my heroes.'

She shook her head. 'A splendid writer, I give you that. Of romances. But he got it all wrong, didn't he?'

Faro looked at her, amazed at her perception. He had read all Scott's books eagerly, avidly, and realized the minute he set foot in Elrigg how far his hero was from the core of truth.

'This is hardly the land of romance, of Gothic mystery as he portrayed it, don't you agree? You just have to be here a few hours to set that right.'

He found himself remembering that her choice of reading lay in the Sensation novels category, when he answered: 'You think the fairy tale of brave gallant Scot and sturdy Celt was a myth?'

'I most certainly do. As were his brave knights and beautiful maidens with high moral principles and dreams of chivalry. Men and women aren't like that. They're flesh and blood – weak creatures.'

'Not all flesh is weak,' he said stoutly.

'Don't tell me you believe all the ballads that are handed down from one generation to the next and form the heart of this nation's poetic soul. Can you be that innocent – or idealistic?'

She laughed and, before he could reply, she added solemnly: 'Scott was a Borderer himself, he must have known the truth, the terror and cruelty that he winced away from writing about. But he opted for the false name of romance to turn a blind eye on reality, on what really happened, and instead was content to present history as a kind of Arthurian legend.'

He knew it was true. Nothing was further from the reivers' thoughts than dying for their God and Queen or King.

'The patriotism Scott believed in never existed,' she said as if she read his thoughts. 'All they knew was the law of the jungle, of every man for himself and the devil take the hindmost. If patriotism of any kind existed, it was well down on their list of priorities.'

She pulled out a piece of grass from the fence and began to shred it. 'Patriotism that men die for – that's a different game, far removed from your fairy tales. Some of us know that only too well.'

He looked at her. The Irish accent she tried to suppress was stronger now, released by her passions.

'You are an authoress, are you not?'

She turned quickly to face him. 'How—'

'Ink stains on your fingernails, a valise full of papers—'

She held up her hand. 'I should have known – you being a policeman. Just my luck,' she murmured, turning away from him again.

'What brings you here?' he asked.

'What do you think? I'm writing a book, of course. One of your dreaded romances,' she said so mockingly he knew it to be a lie.

Staring at the horizon as though seeing a secret pageant of weeping ghosts, her eyes widened. Suddenly she shivered. 'I've had enough of this place. Can we go down now?'

It was a slow, silent journey, step by tortuous step, as she leaned heavily on his arm.

When at last they set foot on the road, she looked pale and exhausted. Faro looked at her anxiously. How was she to manage the long walk to the lodge? The alternative was to carry her.

'Listen,' she said. 'Someone's coming.'

A pony trap bustled round the bend in the road.

Dr Brand stopped, raised his hat, looked from one to the other, smiling.

Miss Crowe limped towards him.

'An accident? Dear, dear.'

As she explained he was already helping her into the cart with Faro's assistance.

'You too, Mr Faro. You're lucky I was along the road. Called out to a difficult birth. Yes, yes, both well and doing fine now. I'll see Miss Crowe safely home, bind up that ankle. I'll set you down at the inn, sir.'

But Faro had spent enough time in Miss Crowe's uncomfortable company. She was impossible. He hadn't changed his original opinion of her and was left quite unmoved by the common bond they shared in his hero, Sir Walter Scott.

As they drove off he was seized by a fit of sneezing. Putting his hand in his greatcoat pocket for a handkerchief, he encountered Miss Crowe's book.

Waving it, he called after them, but they were too distant to heed him.

'Damn and blast,' he said, returning it to his pocket. He sneezed again.

Chapter 14

Faro decided to visit the kirkyard. Vince might laugh at what he called his stepfather's morbid addiction but Faro found that such dalliance in the past had often saved him a considerable amount of walking. Many pieces of information could be gleaned and questions answered where there was no written evidence regarding past inhabitants.

As he walked his attention was drawn to a babble of shrill childish voices. It issued from the playground of the local school and indicated an earnest game of hopscotch.

The sound of a whistle blown by an elderly lady, greyhaired and pince-nezed, imposed immediate silence as the children swiftly formed a crocodile at the school door. Faro applauded the dominie's speedy control over forty or more pupils and he guessed that she had taught and disciplined, stern but kindly, at least two generations of Elrigg children.

Here was a contact worth following, he thought, as he continued on his way to the kirkyard where the lichened tombstones leaned at dangerous angles as if occupants rested uneasily in their graves. Surrounded by ancient cottages, it confirmed his awareness of being under observation. By now, his presence was known to the entire population, his identity a matter of tireless speculation. As, no doubt, was his appearance today with Miss Crowe, and equally distasteful as it might be to both, already interpreted as a budding romance.

At least he would prove them wrong for, in the matter

of Imogen Crowe, nothing was further from his thoughts as he concentrated on the task in hand.

Entering the church by the Norman door, he found himself facing a twelfth-century rounded chancel arch leading to the altar with its handsome rose window.

He knew enough about old churches to hazard a guess that Elrigg St Mary's with its square tower and narrow slit windows in the belfry tower had been built with defence as well as worship in mind, an additional place of security for the priest and worshippers to take refuge from raiders.

Never a religious man, Faro limited his appearances in the kirk of St Giles in Edinburgh to christenings, marriages and funerals but standing before the tiny altar surrounded by these ancient stones brought a feeling of peace and tranquillity, a sense of benediction.

If he had been a praying man, he would have seized the opportunity to beg for an audience, but he felt uncomfortable calling upon God's assistance when he was not a communicant of the Christian church. He looked up at the figure of Christ on the crucifix above the altar and, for one fanciful moment, it seemed that the Son of God's wry expression saw right through him and understood his problems very well indeed.

With a sigh, he wandered over to the stone effigies of the Elriggs who had dominated this piece of Northumberland for more than five hundred years. Elaborately carved and marbled, with a profusion of weeping angels, their tombs told him nothing and he wished, not for the first time, that he had with him his Sergeant, Danny McQuinn of the Edinburgh City Police.

He had never thought the Queen's mission would be simple, but the answers were turning out to be far more difficult than he had imagined. Living at the inn and carrying out inquiries at the Castle without proper authority to do so was fraught with frustrations. He felt that, as always when dealing with the aristocracy, the best clues were to be found in the servants' hall. But he could think of no good excuse for an insurance investigator to be closely questioning them regarding their mistress's behaviour.

This was the area in which McQuinn excelled. The boy who had left Ireland in the disastrous years after the potato famine had grown up to be a man of the people. There was no class barrier for Danny McQuinn. He could be relied upon to ferret out confidences that would never be given, tongue-tied and scared, in the awesome presence of a senior detective inspector. Servants felt at ease with McQuinn with his homely Irish wit, his charm with the humblest of maids, each one of whom he treated like a well-born lady. Such methods would be sure to find a way to get – and to keep – them talking.

Closing the church door behind him, Faro made his way slowly through the tombstones, reading the inscriptions.

'Good day to you, sir!'

The vicar, a tall figure in flowing black robes and white bands, hurried towards him.

'Perhaps I can help you, sir. Are you searching for someone in particular?'

As Faro murmured that he was just interested in old stones, Reverend Cairncross's natural curiosity about this stranger in their midst showed a disarmingly human side to the man of God whose ascetic face and lean frame were that of a medieval monk. His appearance suggested that he had been only recently removed from penning illuminated manuscripts in Melrose Abbey.

'You are, I believe, Mr – Faro – the insurance assessor?'

Thus confronted, Faro did not feel up to the direct lie. Yes indeed, he was here in connection with Sir Archie's death.

That was strictly true.

Reverend Cairncross murmured sympathetically but the word 'death' had injected a sudden chill into his manner. The sudden tightening of his lips and his brooding gaze in the direction of the Castle hinted louder than any words that the Elriggs were not the most popular of his parishioners.

The uncomfortable silence between the two men was

94

broken as a plump middle-aged woman appeared round the side of the church carrying a large basket.

She was introduced as Mrs Cairncross and Faro smiled. The bevy of children at her side indicated the danger of taking people at their face value. The priestly countenance, which suggested monastic celibacy, was gravely in error.

Mrs Cairncross greeted him warmly, talked kindly but anxiously about the weather. These civilities were interrupted as a young woman appeared from the direction of the church gate.

As she was introduced as 'our eldest daughter, Miss Harriet Cairncross', Faro noted that she had inherited her mother's comely looks and curves.

'Are you a bowman, by any chance, Mr Faro?' said Mrs Cairncross.

'Alas, no.'

'A pity,' said her husband, eyeing him narrowly. 'You have an excellent sturdy frame, strong about the shoulders—'

Mrs Cairncross interrupted laughingly, 'Alfred is a great enthusiast. He won the coveted Gold Arrow three years ago and has never forgotten it. I almost said it went to his head,' she giggled helplessly and Reverend Cairncross patted her arm affectionately.

'I can recommend archery to you, sir. A grand healthy relaxation and I tell myself much more in keeping with the Bible than guns.'

'Even if you are not an archer, sir, you must come to the fête in the church hall afterwards,' insisted Mrs Cairncross.

'Mr Faro is an insurance assessor, my dear. He is engaged at the Castle at present.'

Faro observed that the vicar's grip on his wife's arm tightened perceptibly. His words, spoken lightly but with a hint of warning, suddenly changed the scene from being warm and welcoming. It was as if a chill wind had blown over the little group. The daughter stepped back as if taking refuge, hiding behind her mother, and Faro's quick ears detected a strangled sob from the girl as her father bowed a dismissal in his direction.

Seizing her arm as if to restrain her from flight, his head close to hers, chiding or comforting, he propelled her in the direction of the manse.

Mrs Cairncross darted a helpless look at the pair of them, turned to Faro, opened her mouth as if to say something and, unable to think of anything to fit the occasion, turned on her heel and hurried after them.

Left standing, Faro regarded their swift departure thoughtfully. Curious behaviour indeed, remembering that warning tone clear as a bell as he was being introduced by the vicar to his wife and pretty daughter.

As he continued his perusal of the tombstones he stored away in his excellent memory the picture of the consternation that the vicar's words 'at the Castle' had struck. A chord that the ominous words 'Detective Inspector Faro' normally aroused in those whose consciences trembled with guilt.

Now he wondered what the Cairncross family had to hide. Their reactions could hardly have been more dramatic had they known his real identity. The blight that mention of Elriggs or Castle brought into the most friendly and ordinary conversations was becoming uncomfortably familiar, swiftly changing listeners' attitudes from geniality to suspicious alertness, tense and watchful as the wild cattle on the hill.

Experienced as he was in the nuances of criminal attitudes, such strange behaviour fascinated him, as he wondered how many more village folk would be thrown into panic and consternation by the innocent announcement of his business at Elrigg.

Continuing his inspection of the gravestones, which was proving singularly uneventful, he was once again seized by a fit of sneezing. Aware of being tired and hoping this was not the prelude to a fever, he sat down on a rustic seat sheltered by the church wall.

Taking out his handkerchief, he encountered the book

Miss Crowe had dropped. *The History of Civilization* by Henry Thomas Buckle. A curious choice, he thought, for a young woman whose main reading was of the sensational kind. Opening it at the bookmarked page he read:

Of all offences, it might well be supposed that the crime of murder is one of the most arbitrary and irregular. For when we consider that this, though generally the crowning act of a long career of vice, is often the immediate result of what seems a sudden impulse; *that when premeditated, its committal, even with the least change of impunity, requires a rare combination of favourable circumstances, for which the criminal will frequently wait; that he has thus to bide his time and look for opportunities he cannot control, that when the time has come his heart may fail him,* that the question whether or not he shall commit the crime may depend on a balance of conflicting motives, such as fear of the law, a dread of penalties held out by religion, the prickings of his own conscience, the apprehension of future remorse, the love of gain, jealousy, revenge, desperation; – when we put all these things together, there arises such a complication of causes, that we might reasonably despair of detecting any order or method in the result of those subtle and shifting agencies by which murder is either caused or prevented. But now, how stands the fact. The fact is, that murder is committed with as much regularity, and bears as uniform a relation to certain known circumstances, as do the movements of the tides, and the rotations of the seasons.

Faro re-read the lines heavily underscored and, turning back the pages, read the owner's name on the flyleaf, so unexpected and disturbing that it set at naught all his evidence. With a sickening feeling of dismay he realized he might well have been following the wrong track.

97

Chapter 15

Faro walked slowly down the main street, wrestling with the enormity of his new discovery. Constable Dewar had to hail him twice before he was aware of an interruption to his dismal thoughts.

The constable was off-duty, in his garden opposite the police station. With considerable effort Faro returned his greeting and paused to admire the neat array of daffodils.

Dewar smiled, indicating the rustic seat by the door.

'You're looking tired, sir. Rest yourself a while. Mrs Dewar'll bring us out a drink while we enjoy the sunshine.'

Faro needed no second invitation. As he sat down with a sigh of relief, Dewar said: 'Inquiries going well, sir?'

Faro shook his head. He didn't have McQuinn but in the circumstances Constable Dewar, who had lived in Elrigg for many years, might have convenient access to the kind of information he needed.

He sighed. 'Not very well, I'm afraid. I could do with your help, Constable.'

Dewar looked startled at the request. He regarded Faro indecisively, and then, squaring his shoulders, said firmly: 'I'll be straight with you, sir, although I don't think you're being straight with me.'

While Faro was thinking of a suitably evasive reply, he continued: 'I've been keeping an eye on your activities, sir.' He paused dramatically, 'You're a policeman yourself, aren't you?'

Taking Faro's silence as affirmation, he smiled triumphantly.

'You're either a policeman or you have been at some time in your life.'

At Faro's grudging admission, Dewar thumped his fists together with a crow of delight.

'Knew I was right all along, sir. Said so to Sergeant Yarrow. All he says is that if you wanted us to know that, then you'd tell us. And that I was to keep quiet about what I suspected.'

As Faro wondered anxiously how many others Dewar might have confided his suspicions to, the constable leaned forward and said earnestly: 'I am at your service, sir. You can rely on PC Dewar. Born and bred in the place, there's nothing I don't know about the ways of folk hereabouts. Elrigg's an open book to me,' he added proudly.

Faro smiled vaguely.

'What is it exactly your lot sent you down to investigate?'

There seemed little to lose and much to gain by being honest with Dewar and Faro decided to reveal his true identity.

Dewar's eyes boggled. He whistled. 'Not *the* Inspector Faro. From the Edinburgh Police. Well, I never,' he said with an admiring glance. 'Why, every policeman from here to London has heard of you.'

And when Faro bowed modestly, Dewar's expression changed to one of shrewd intelligence.

'Then it must be something very important indeed that's brought you here. Not a couple of missing paintings or a death insurance, I'll be bound.'

Faro frowned. 'I take it that you are aware of who was Sir Archie's companion on the day of his accident?'

Dewar beamed. 'Bless you, sir, everyone does. Although we all pretend to go along with their incognitos. "Mr Osbourne" – a lot of nonsense.'

'Tell me, is there much security attached to these visits?'

'Security!' Dewar laughed. 'At Elrigg? Bless your heart, no, sir. Sergeant Yarrow and I are required to ride at a

99

discreet distance. This isn't London or Edinburgh, not like any big city. Just a token presence of the law, you understand, where royal visitors are concerned.

'We know all the people here, you see, and if there was any villain coming in with bad intent, well, he'd stand out like a sore thumb, sir. We'd be on to him before he had time to know what hit him.'

Even as Faro doubted that, he remembered his aunt's similar reaction to the Deeside inhabitants in the vicinity of Balmoral Castle.

'People think they are just strangers passing through and won't be noticed. They'd think differently if they knew how newcomers are a fascinating topic of speculation. Of course,' Dewar continued, tapping the side of his nose with his forefinger, 'we all know the real reason for the royal gentleman's visit, but enough said.'

And he closed his mouth firmly, loyal to Queen or Prince and Country.

'Where do you get your information from?' Faro asked.

'Servants, sir,' said Dewar cheerfully. 'The way the gentleman in question has to have a room nearby his, er, interest, if you get my meaning. So that he can come and go without embarrassment to either of them . . .'

Faro's eyes widened to think that matters arranged with such delicacy by discreet aristocratic hosts were in fact common village gossip.

Dewar paused and then, in a tone purposely diffident, 'Her Ladyship's a rum 'un, mind you.' And again he regarded Faro nervously and closed his mouth firmly in the way of a man who fears he has already said more than enough.

'How so?' Faro prodded him gently.

Dewar took a deep breath. 'Well, sir, the class she comes from, actresses and such like. Can't see one of her kind settling down to be a proper wife to His Lordship. Stands to reason, his family's one of the oldest in the land, older than any royalty.' With a shake of his head he added pityingly, 'Her so young, five years married and not a bairn, much less an heir. Just ain't natural.'

'Presumably Sir Archie wasn't worried by this?'

'You can never tell with that class of people, sir.'

'He does have an heir, I gather.'

'Yes, Mark, his first wife's son. But it's not the same, is it, sir?'

'I understood that they were close kin.'

'Yes.' Dewar sounded doubtful. 'The first Lady Elrigg was Sir Archie's cousin, so the lad had a right by blood. I was one of the witnesses to the will, sir, I tell you that in confidence. That in the event of the laird dying without issue, it would all go to Mark.'

Dewar frowned for a moment, before saying in the manner of one choosing his words carefully: 'It seems to me that Lady Elrigg isn't as grieved as is natural in the circumstances. Not like the example Her Majesty has set for widowed ladies. She's ordered mourning to be set aside and I hear tell that she and her companion have been heard playing the piano, singing comic songs. Now that's not nice.'

At Dewar's shocked expression Faro said gently: 'You mustn't forget that the two ladies are very young. At least having a companion who has known her a long time must be a great help to Lady Elrigg at this time.'

'That's as maybe,' Dewar admitted grudgingly, 'But Miss Kent doesn't behave like a servant at all. Very grand with everyone in the village, too. Too good for the likes of us, you'd think. And it's time she was finding herself a man before it's too late . . .'

Faro felt a fleeting sympathy for Miss Kent at the village matchmakers' mercy as Dewar went on: 'Bowden tells me that one or two of his customers – young lads – have made, well, advances when she's been down on an errand. Nothing coarse or undesirable, you understand,' he added hastily, 'just friendly – a bit saucy like they are with the maids at the Castle. But this one just gives them a steely look, a frosty reply.

'What can you expect with stage folk?' He shook his head. 'Can't be doing with them. Mind you, I was sorry for

101

that poor actor chap who had that nasty accident while staying at the Castle.'

'What kind of accident?' Faro asked innocently.

'Well, sir, it was all a bit mysterious, if you ask me. If it had happened anywhere else there would have been a full inquiry but here, well, it seemed to me that it was very hastily hushed up, the Chief Constable and the Coroner being close kin of Sir Archie—'

'Wait a moment,' Faro interrupted. 'You mean that there was something to hush up – like foul play?'

'Well,' said Dewar reluctantly, 'that's what I thought.'

'How so?'

Dewar shrugged. 'This actor arrives in the village and takes a room at the inn. He starts asking about Her Ladyship. Seems he was an old chum, they have been on the boards in London. Next thing we knew, he's cleared off in a carriage taking him to the Castle, to be the guest of the Elriggs, to entertain Mr Osbourne – on one of his visits. Must have been there for about a week, when he and Mr Osbourne went out riding together.'

He paused, frowning. 'Mr Osbourne came back alone, so we were told. They had parted company. No one took much notice of the fact that Mr Gray was missing at dinner that evening. It wasn't until next morning, when the maids discovered his bed hadn't been slept in, that the alarm was raised. The servants were a bit worried about that, especially the housekeeper, who thought he'd maybe gone off with the silver. You can never tell with that class of people, sir.

'We were alerted but we weren't permitted to question Mr Osbourne personally. All we had was what he told His Lordship, that he and Mr Gray had ridden as far as the pastureland at the edge of the estate and he, Mr Osbourne, was feeling tired and decided to return.

'That was all we had to go on. We set out and there he was, poor gentleman, lying dead in the copse beside the hillfort. He'd been gored by one of the wild cattle. There was no doubt about that. A dreadful accident. The Coroner and Sir Archie were all for having it cleared as quickly as possible. Didn't want it getting into the newspapers, with royalty involved.'

He looked at Faro. 'I've often thought that it was odd finding His Lordship in the same place. Died the same way too. A strange coincidence, don't you think?'

Faro made no comment, thinking that any other police than Elrigg would have thought it also suspicious enough to merit immediate investigation.

At that moment they were interrupted as Mrs Dewar came out of the house, drying her hands on her apron.

'Food's ready, Sandy.' And, seeing Faro, she smiled. 'Is this the gentleman you were telling me about?'

She bobbed a curtsy as they were introduced, looking very impressed. 'Won't you take a bite to eat with us, sir?'

'Aye, do that,' said Dewar. 'Jessie can beat the inn for anything they might produce. And it's steak pie—'

'Go on with you, Sandy,' said Mrs Dewar. 'Can't have Mr Faro expecting too much. It's all simple food.'

As they led the way into the house, he heard her murmur to her husband, 'He's younger than I thought he'd be. And my, isn't he handsome?'

Chapter 16

Faro ate at the Dewars' kitchen table with its welcoming fire and even more welcoming smell of freshly baked pies. The vacant place opposite him was set for Sergeant Yarrow, the constable explained: 'We don't have many meals together. I go on duty when he comes off so that the station is manned during the day. He boards with us, has the spare room upstairs. House is too big for Jessie and me since the lads left the nest.'

'Came to look for a place of his own. But somehow he just stayed on and we've got used to having him.' Mrs Dewar looked round from piling extra potatoes on their plates. 'He's such a nice kind thoughtful man. Just like one of the family. More pie, Mr Faro?'

Faro declined the offer and Mrs Dewar continued: 'He's not a bit of trouble. He'd make a grand husband for some lucky lady, I tell him.'

Dewar laughed. 'Jessie's always trying to marry him off. There's no such thing as single blessedness for her.'

'A crime against nature, that's what it is, God never meant his creatures to live solitary lives,' Mrs Dewar protested.

'A bachelor, is he?' said Faro.

'Not him, more's the pity. His wife died around the time of his accident.'

'Aye, and he misses her. I often see him looking at her photograph when I take him in his tea,' sighed Mrs Dewar. 'I think he was glad to start a new life here, away from all the memories.'

Pausing, she looked across the table at Faro. 'Are you a married man yourself?'

Faro shook his head. 'Like your Sergeant, I'm a widower. My wife died in childbirth eight years ago.'

'How sad,' tut-tutted Mrs Dewar. 'You're all alone too, sir?'

'Not quite. I have two little girls living with their granny up in Orkney.'

'Orkney?' Mrs Dewar frowned. 'That's a fair distance from Edinburgh, isn't it?'

Faro smiled. 'It is indeed. But my wife was married before and I have a stepson living with me. He's a doctor.'

'That's nice for you. You'll have another spoonful of dumpling?'

'Yes, thank you, Mrs Dewar. That was absolutely delicious.'

As Mrs Dewar beamed, very liberal with the jam sauce, they heard the back door open.

'Talk of the devil,' said Dewar. 'That's the Sergeant now. I'll need to take over, Jessie,' he added, scraping his plate.

Faro wished he could have had a moment in private with Dewar to stress the need for secrecy. He didn't want the news of his real identity spread around Elrigg. However, such a hurried exit was impossible with a second helping of pudding uneaten on his plate.

Sergeant Yarrow's greeting was friendly and politely interested as he enquired about the progress of Faro's investigations. As Mrs Dewar made a great deal of fuss over him, he seemed to enjoy her attentions.

Faro mentioned that he had been to the kirkyard and Yarrow said: 'If you're interested in the history of Elrigg and the cattle, I have a book upstairs. You can borrow it if you like. It won't take long to read.'

'What about your food, Sergeant?' Mrs Dewar sounded alarmed.

Yarrow smiled at her. 'That can wait a wee while, Mrs Dewar. I had a pint of ale at the inn so I won't starve.'

'You should be careful. Drinking isn't good for you. I hope you're taking the medicine that Dr Brand gave you.'

'Faithfully, Mrs Dewar.'

Faro looked at him quickly. His colour was bad, he looked like a sick man. And he found himself remembering Imogen Crowe's gloomy pronouncement.

'The Sergeant has one of the best views over Elrigg. A lovely room, it is,' said Mrs Dewar.

'Yes. My window looks directly towards the standing stones and if I take out my telescope, I can watch the cattle grazing. From a safe distance.'

'Why don't you show Mr Faro?'

When Yarrow frowned, Mrs Dewar said, 'No need to worry, it's all neat and tidy, not like the way you left it.'

Yarrow's smile was a little long-suffering as he nodded to Faro. 'Come along then.'

Faro followed him upstairs. The room with its bay window was very attractive, much lighter than the kitchen downstairs. He guessed that Yarrow strove to keep it as a man's domain despite his landlady's feminine touches of lace and vases of flowers.

Yarrow read his expression. 'They're very good to me. It's a relief to have a good working relationship with Dewar – makes life much easier.' He sighed. 'Too easy really. I didn't mean to stay with them year after year. Mrs Dewar spoils me, as you've probably observed.'

Faro was looking at the mantelpiece, dominated by three silver framed photographs. A wedding – a younger, handsome Yarrow in Metropolitan Police uniform with his pretty bride; a second photograph of the couple staring down at a baby and a third of Mrs Yarrow with a handsome curly-haired infant on her knee, smiling into the camera.

'What a beautiful child. Yours?' said Faro.

'Yes. But no more, alas.' Yarrow turned from the glass fronted bookcase, his face expressionless. 'This is the book. No hurry, just leave it at the inn for me when you go—'

'Your food's getting cold, Sergeant!'

At Mrs Dewar's call upstairs, Faro smiled. 'I'll be on my way,' and he hurried downstairs through the kitchen, thanking Mrs Dewar for her kindness while she urged him to drop in any time.

'You'll be most welcome to share our little meal with us.'

He was not sorry to have missed eating at the Elrigg Arms in what would have been solitary splendour. A few farmers with their dogs occupied the bar and Bowden stopped him on his way up to his room. 'You've missed your visitor, sir.' At Faro's puzzled expression Bowden laughed. 'Aye, Jack Duffy. Called in to see you on the off-chance.'

'What did he want?'

'Wouldn't say. Just that he wanted a word with you. In a right old state he was, said it was urgent and where were you, and so forth. I told him I wasn't your keeper—'

'Did he leave a note?'

'A note, sir. Duffy can't write. There's nothing wrong with his sums though. He can certainly add up.' Bowden grinned. 'It was something important he wanted to get off his chest, that's for sure.' Bowden gave Faro a significant wink. 'And knowing Duffy, like I told you, I'd take any bet you like that it has to do with money.'

'Did he say when he'd be back?'

'Told me to tell you he'd be in at six again tomorrow evening. I was to tell you to be here because he had vital information to give you.'

Faro felt exasperated at having missed the poacher a second time. Was it no more than a ruse to extract money from a stranger by offering him some stolen booty, or did he know something vital about Sir Archie's death that he was willing to sell to the insurance mannie?

Later that afternoon, Faro set off for the Castle. On his way through the village, his conscience prompted him that he should send a postcard to his daughters in Orkney and write a long overdue letter to his mother.

Opposite the one church which catered for all Elrigg's spiritual needs was the one shop which catered for all their material ones, from food to farming implements.

Purchases in hand, Faro waited for some time behind a customer buying boiled sweets from a large selection of glass jars. Her choice involved a great deal of indecision.

Turning to him, she smiled apologetically and he recognized the elderly schoolteacher, whom the shopkeeper addressed very civilly as Miss Halliday.

'My apologies, sir, these are rewards for good conduct and good marks for my children. Yes, that will do nicely, thank you.' As she awaited the weighing out and summing up of pennies, she continued: 'Are you enjoying your visit? I observed you outside the school railings and deduced that as you were not a parent and therefore known to me personally, you must be a visitor.'

'I am indeed,' Faro smiled inwardly. What splendid detectives these local people would have made. His strict rules of observation and deduction might well have been invented by them.

The teacher obviously expected some further enlightenment and Faro found it difficult to give the kind of response that the woman's shrewd and eager expression demanded. He still wore his recently acquired *persona* like an ill-fitting suit of clothes, about which he was becoming increasingly uncomfortable and self-conscious. A poor actor, he was certain that everyone in Elrigg had seen through his disguise and knew it for a lie.

'If you are staying for a while, perhaps you would care to come to our charity concert, the day after the Archery Contest? The children are performing well-known scenes from Shakespeare's plays and I can guarantee an evening of lively entertainment . . .'

As she warmed to her subject, waxing ecstatic about her small actors and actresses, Faro listened bleakly. How he dreaded and assiduously avoided amateur theatricals, the worst of all being school plays. His role of fond and indulgent parent had its limitations and he was thankful that his daughters Rose and Emily had never exhibited even hints of latent acting abilities.

Thanking Miss Halliday graciously but remaining vague about his immediate future in Elrigg, he made his escape.

Relying on his forged credentials and the fact that the further inquiries of an insurance investigator might be accepted as natural, Faro walked briskly towards the Castle.

At the lodge Imogen Crowe was at home, busily hanging curtains in the kitchen window. Pretending not to notice, and staring hard in the opposite direction, he hurried past, head down, eager to avoid any further communication with her.

An impossible woman.

Chapter 17

The day was warm and sunny and Faro concentrated on what he was going to say to Lady Elrigg and her stepson. The aged butler opened the door and looked down his sharp nose at Faro. As usual he was left waiting on the doorstep for some time while the old man enquired as to who might be at home.

It was all very tiresome, thought Faro, his good nature evaporating rapidly as he wondered if his presence had been forgotten.

At last the door was reopened. 'Her Ladyship is not at home but Mr Mark is willing to see you.'

Faro was relieved to see Mark appear behind the butler at that moment.

'Good day to you, Mr Faro. Shall we stroll in the gardens?'

Faro smiled. Perhaps it was crediting the young man with too much subtlety to have realized that emotions are easier concealed strolling in a garden than sitting face to face across a table. And a much less unnerving experience.

'The paintings haven't turned up, I'm afraid,' Mark volunteered.

Faro would have been surprised if they had, having long since determined their fate.

'I suppose you have documents for us to sign?' Mark continued.

Faro hadn't thought of that.

'Sir Archie didn't tell me – as you know. All a bit of a shock, what happened.'

'I'm sorry. You were close to him,' Faro said boldly.

Mark shrugged. 'As close as anyone. He was good to me and I enjoyed better relations with him than most,' he added frankly.

'He could be a devil sometimes, you know, he believed in the old traditions of the gentry, tried to run Elrigg like a medieval warlord. He refused to believe that times were changing. He yearned for the old-style barony courts, with absolute power of life and death, the *droit de seigneur* – all that sort of thing. He liked the idea of summoning his tenants once a quarter – to dispense justice and administer punishment.'

They had reached the edge of the walled garden. Ahead of them stretched a large expanse of boggy, heavily weeded marshland, quite out of keeping with the neat paths and well-trimmed garden.

'That was once an ornamental lake. We used to sail boats on it, have picnics. Then there was an accident, a girl drowned. Sir Archie wouldn't tolerate that sort of thing on his land. Had it drained. He was like that.'

'It must have been very distressing for you finding him that day – ' Faro decided to pretend ignorance and the mild curiosity that might be expected of him regarding Sir Archie's death.

Mark shook his head. 'I didn't know what had happened until later. I was busy in the estate office. Something my stepfather wanted checked,' he continued swiftly. Then, looking at Faro, he said, 'We were used to him being unseated by his horse. He would arrive back on foot in a towering rage, out for blood.'

'That happened often?'

'Often enough. He had a passion for highly bred Arab horses, very expensive. He had to show them – like everyone else – that he was master. Used the whip cruelly at the breaking-in process—'

'He was riding alone, I take it?'

'No. As a matter of fact he had one of our guests with him.'

'And didn't this guest give the alarm?'

'Of course,' said Mark uncomfortably. 'Oh, there you are,' he called as Lady Elrigg and her companion Miss Kent emerged from the walled garden, the relief in his voice suggesting rescue from a particularly nasty situation.

Faro bowed politely, greeted them cordially. While he listened to Mark explaining too brightly that Mr Faro was still busy with his inquiries about the paintings, he felt that Lady Elrigg's smile was fixed and held no warmth.

But it was the companion who most interested him. This was their first meeting and he regarded her with considerable interest in the light of Constable Dewar's scathing remarks regarding her matrimonial chances.

Beatrice Kent was tall and thin with a sallow complexion, the kind of anonymity that doomed actresses to character roles. Even in extreme youth he doubted whether she had ever been pretty enough for juvenile leads. She was no foil for her mistress's flamboyant beauty.

She was aware of his scrutiny and turned aside sharply. At her side Poppy Elrigg continued to smile, her composure unimpaired by this encounter with the insurance assessor. Only Miss Kent showed evidence of despair, her lips trembling, her eyes darting back and forth nervously from one to the other as if in some desperate mute appeal for help.

At last she touched Lady Elrigg's arm, the slightest gesture but enough communication for the two women to turn and look at him with expressions that left him in no doubt regarding his popularity. And had they been able to slip back into the shrubbery unobserved he guessed they would have withdrawn immediately.

Feeling that words of explanation were demanded of him, he said heartily: 'Just the usual procedures, you know.'

'In view of our unfortunate bereavement, I was reminding him – ' Mark's voice held a note of pleading.

'I'm sure Mr Faro understands perfectly.' Lady Elrigg's

112

brilliant smile in his direction was followed by a brisk nod to Mark. 'And now, if you'll excuse us. Come along, Mark,' she added as if he had some burning desire to remain. 'Beatrice and I were looking for you. There are estate matters urgently needing your attention, you know.'

The heir to Elrigg seemed in no great hurry to take over his duties either and Faro, detecting a hint of reproach and reprimand, regarded their rapid exit thoughtfully.

Lady Elrigg had been particularly anxious to remove Mark and, he felt sure, she would be very concerned about the particulars of their conversation.

At that moment, he decided that Mark was the most unlikely person to have murdered Sir Archie if he had found him unconscious in the spinney.

Unless he was lying in wait for just such a possibility, when he most certainly would have been seen in the vicinity by Yarrow or Dewar. Besides, from what Mark had told him, Faro felt the boy was more likely to have rushed to the scene and tried his best to resuscitate his stepfather.

Returning along the Castle drive, deep in his own thoughts, Faro stepped aside to make way for a rider leading a string of horses.

Greetings exchanged, Faro was admiring the mare with her new foal, when the lad said: 'You're the man from the insurance people. I thought I recognized you. I've seen you at the inn.'

'You were here the day of His Lordship's accident?'

'I was that,' said the lad as he dismounted. 'Mind you, I thought little of it at the time. His Lordship had frequent disagreements with the beasts. Often came off worst.'

He shook his head. 'I didn't realize he was hurt, especially as the other gentleman rode in, never mentioned it—'

'This other gentleman. Who was he?'

The stable boy gave him a curious look. 'Very important he was sir, very confidential. We'd lose our jobs if we

113

talked about him – gossiped and the like,' he said anxiously.

'Quite so. I just wondered why he hadn't waited and seen His Lordship home.'

'Can't say, sir. He rode in, I helped him dismount and he was very wet and in a tearing rage, I could see that. He ordered his carriage to be sent round immediately and stormed off to the house. We hadn't been told that he was leaving and of course there was the usual panic. I watched him leave with his servants, wondering about His Lordship. Wasn't like him not to be there to speed on the departing guest. Her Ladyship looked a bit flustered, apologetic like.'

'Was Mr Mark with her?'

'No. I didn't see him. When I got back to the stables, His Lordship's horse galloped in. I was alarmed. I realized His Lordship might have gone right up to the Castle not to be late for dinner. But that wasn't like him. It was still raining and getting dark. I chatted to the other lads and none of us liked the idea of him lying hurt out there, especially with the cattle roaming about, upset by a stalking party earlier on. And we'd been told there were some young calves just dropped.

'Then Constable Dewar rode in, told us about the accident.' He shrugged. 'When we got there it was too late. Sergeant Yarrow and Dr Brand were with him.'

'Anyone else?'

The stable lad thought. 'Aye. Mr Mark and Mr Hector were standing about and one or two of the estate folk. But there wasn't anything they could do.'

As Faro continued on his way, he made a mental picture of the scene in the copse. Mark, Hector and a few anonymous 'estate folk', any of whom could ride a horse and might have found Sir Archie lying injured. From what he had learned, all the tenants were expert archers. It didn't take much stretch of imagination to realize that the bull's horn might be used as a murder weapon.

He considered the time factor. Although it took the

114

best part of thirty minutes to walk briskly to the copse from the Castle, ten minutes on a swift mount was all that was required, taking well-known short cuts over fields and fences.

Luck had been with the murderer since Sergeant Yarrow's arrival had been delayed by his horse going lame. A murderer who was clever – or desperate – who had discovered the bull's horns and realized the possibilities of re-enacting the death of the actor Philip Gray by blaming it on the wild cattle.

His thoughts were irresistibly drawn once more to Hector Elrigg. He could not dismiss him from his list of possible suspects. He spent most of his working days at the hillfort with the copse in clear view, his cottage less than a hundred yards away.

And Hector was an expert archer.

Chapter 18

Deep in thought, Faro was halfway between the Castle drive and the village when the rain began. A few preliminary warning spots became a torrential downpour. Taking refuge in the only available shelter offered by a large but still leafless oak tree whose branches hung over the estate wall, he gazed longingly towards a cottage on the other side of the road.

Smoke issued from its chimney bringing the scent of a peat fire. Lamplight gleamed in its windows. Suddenly the door opened and a lady beckoned to him.

'Won't you come and take shelter, sir? It is only a shower, and it will soon pass . . .'

Faro recognized the schoolteacher Miss Halliday. And needing no second bidding, he raced across the intervening ground and followed her into the kitchen where a kettle whistled merrily on a large fire.

The room was well filled with bookshelves, every inch of wall covered by framed paintings, every foot of floor by sofas and soft-cushioned chairs. The hands of the needle-woman, either her own or those of her pupils, had been industriously employed through the years.

She pointed to the kettle. 'I was about to make myself a cup of tea when I looked out of the window, thinking my poor plants – how they would welcome a drink. And there you were, poor gentleman – getting absolutely drenched. Perhaps you would like a cup of tea while we try to dry you off.'

Faro insisted that he wasn't very wet, thanks to her

timely intervention, but the tea would be most welcome.

As he introduced himself as Mr Faro, Miss Halliday smiled wordlessly and held out her hands for his coat. 'Wait a moment till I set a place for you at the table – oh yes, I insist,' she said and, indicating the papers she bundled on to the sideboard: 'Two of our little girls, sisters, have gone down with scarlet fever. Most unfortunate, the poor dears. I have to fill these in for Sergeant Yarrow.' She sighed. 'I do hope we don't have to be quarantined and our little school closed.'

Faro murmured sympathetically as she set before him a plate of scones.

'By my cookery class,' she said proudly. 'They are quite excellent. Do try them.'

His initial misgivings were quickly set aside and he accepted a second helping.

She looked pleased. 'The dear children, all of them have their own special gift, there isn't one of them who doesn't shine at something. If they aren't clever at sums then they are usually very good with their hands. Do you have children, sir?'

Faro told her about Emily and Rose and she listened, smiling, and nodded sympathetically when she heard he was a widower.

'I can tell you are very proud of your daughters, a pity they cannot live in Edinburgh with you, but I think you have made the right decision, the countryside is a much better and safer choice for children to grow up in. Won't you come and sit by the fire?'

As he sank into a comfortable chair, he sighed. 'What a pretty house you have, Miss Halliday.' Noticing how some of her movements were slow and rheumatic, he added, 'Would it not be more convenient to live on the school house premises?'

She laughed. 'I know what you're thinking, Mr Faro, a big barn of a house for one elderly lady without any servants. But you see this has always been my home. I was born in this house, so were my parents and grandparents.

It was a farmhouse in those days. Do you know, Sir Walter Scott once stayed here,' she added proudly. 'We have his letter.' And she pointed to a framed letter among the many watercolours.

'How fascinating, Miss Halliday. Why, Sir Walter is one of my heroes. I've read all his books.'

'And so have I. Well, he most likely sat on that very same chair you are occupying now, Mr Faro. Here you are – ' and so saying she took down the letter. 'Read it – aloud, if you please, I love to hear his words.'

Touching through the glass that well-beloved hand-writing which had brought him so many hours of pleasure, Faro began:

Behold a letter from the mountain, for I am very snugly settled here in a farmer's house, about six miles from Wooler, in the very centre of the Cheviot Hills, in one of the wildest and most romantic situations . . . To add to my satisfaction we are midst places renowned by the feats of former days; each hill is crowned with a tower, or camp, or cairn; and in no situation can you be nearer more fields of battle. Out of the brooks with which these hills are intersected, we pull trouts of half a yard in length and we are in the very country of muir fowl. My uncle drinks the goat's whey here as I do ever since I understood it was brought to his bedside every morning at six by a very pretty dairy maid—

'Stop a moment, sir,' Miss Halliday interrupted, her face gleaming with excitement. 'That dairy maid was my great-grandmother. Sir Walter was only twenty years old when he wrote that. He was still a law clerk in his father's office.'

She sighed happily. 'I like to think that he might have been a little in love with that pretty girl. I do beg your pardon, sir, please continue.'

All the day we shoot, fish, walk and ride; dine and sup on fish struggling from the stream, and the most delicious health-fed mutton, barn door fowls, pies, mild-cheese, etc. all in perfection: and so much simplicity resides among these hills that a pen, which could write at least, was not to be found about the house, though belonging to a considerable farmer, till I shot the crow with whose quill I write this epistle.

Miss Halliday sighed. 'Thank you, sir. I do so love to hear a man's voice read that letter, although I know every word of it. And you did it so nicely.' And rehanging it, she added: 'I like to think that perhaps he found his inspiration as a great author while staying in this house. I have been very fortunate today.' She smiled.

'Indeed?'

'Yes, I must confess that you are the second person who has so indulged me. A young lady, Miss Crowe.' She shook her head. 'A young lady of mystery, I might add. She comes and she goes. Perhaps you have met her? She lives at the Castle lodge.'

'She occasionally takes meals at the inn where I am staying.'

'Does she really?' said Miss Halliday eagerly. 'And what do you think of her?'

'I really haven't paid her much attention, to be honest.'

As Miss Halliday refilled the teapot, Faro sensed that she was disappointed with his answer, and that she would have very much enjoyed a little speculative gossip about the mysterious Miss Crowe.

Faro, however, was more keenly interested in the treasures that surrounded him, the walls with their watercolours. Photographs too, for this new fashion had obviously seized Miss Halliday's enthusiasm.

There were several paintings of pretty young children and in place of honour an outstanding watercolour portrait of a handsome young boy who stared out at them with large enquiring eyes and a slight shy smile. He seemed ready to speak, his expression reminding Faro of someone he had met recently.

'One of your paintings, Miss Halliday?'

She clasped her hands in delight. 'Indeed yes, I'm glad you approve of my little painting.'

'A relation perhaps?'

He expected to be told that this was indeed a favourite nephew but instead she shook her head sadly.

'Merely a favourite pupil.' She sighed. 'Poor dear little Eric, he was at the school a few years ago, and I must confess that he was exactly like the son I would have wished for had I ever married.'

She paused and Faro asked: 'Where is he now? Grown up and away, I expect.'

'If only that were so.' She bit her lip and turned away, near to tears and Faro guessed the answer before she spoke.

'He is dead, sir. Killed on the estate here, a most tragic accident. He was with the young beaters, when a gun that one of the party was loading misfired.'

She shook her head, her eyes tragic. 'We could hardly believe such a thing could happen. You can imagine how everyone felt, we were heartbroken – guilty even, for the boy was only a visitor but we were all fond of him, he had made so many friends. And, of course, we all blamed ourselves for not taking better care of him.'

Faro looked at her. Loyalty obviously demanded discretion and according to Hector Elrigg, the gun had been in the hands of Sir Archie who had been drunk at the time.

As he was leaving, he realized sadly that this handsome young boy who had won his way into her spinsterly heart and tragically died had been Miss Halliday's nearest encounter with motherhood.

But the person the boy reminded him of remained stubbornly obscure.

Chapter 19

Six o'clock was wheezing from the inn's ancient clock as Faro sat down to his supper. The dining room was empty and he was well pleased that he had the table to himself for his meeting with Duffy. He would put a pint of ale in front of the poacher just to loosen his tongue a little, with hopes that this eagerness for a meeting signalled enlightenment on the mystery of Sir Archie's last hours.

But his meal was finished, seven had struck with no sign of Duffy, and Faro returned to the bar where Bowden, polishing the counter with his usual eagerness, did not share his anxiety.

'Not the most reliable of chaps,' he said. 'If something better comes along, isn't that so, Sergeant?' he asked Yarrow who was seated at the far end of the counter.

Yarrow's wry smile indicated that Duffy was not one of his favourites. 'Care to join me, Mr Faro?'

Faro did so but with some diffidence since the bar was directly overlooked by a window. If Duffy chanced to look in and saw the insurance mannie chatting to the law in the shape of Yarrow, this might well scare him off.

As time passed in desultory talk with the Sergeant, Faro was certain this must have happened, despite his efforts to keep a watchful eye on the door.

At last Yarrow buttoned up his tunic and announced that he was back on duty. Faro was relieved to see him depart and with a final word to Bowden to let him know when Duffy arrived, he prepared to go up to his room.

The barman shook his head and looked at the clock.

'You'll not see him tonight, sir, he'll be busy about his own business by now. He'll have forgotten all about your arrangement and he'll be in as usual for his pint of ale at opening time tomorrow morning. If he's sober enough to walk, that is.'

Faro spent the rest of the evening making notes, bringing his log of the case up to date, carefully writing in dossiers of what he knew of the suspects, and of their movements.

Conscious that such an investigation had never been his responsibility and that he had no legal right to interfere, he threw down his pen at last.

The time had come to reveal his identity and confide his suspicions to Sergeant Yarrow. The rest was up to the Northumberland Constabulary who might well consider his observations of merely academic interest. If they felt there was not enough at this late date to follow his leads and reopen an inquiry into Sir Archie's death, he had done what he considered his moral duty.

When he undertook the Queen's Command regarding the future King of England, he had not expected to be landed with a murder case. In fact, the only conclusion he had reached was that the person least likely to have murdered Sir Archie was the Prince of Wales, despite his suspiciously hurried departure from Elrigg Castle.

Whether he had been guilty of that gravest of British sins, cowardice, could, however, be settled only by that most unsatisfactory of Scottish verdicts: 'Not proven'.

Faro slept badly that night, haunted by his old nightmare. Pursued by Highland cattle, the bull's hot breath on his heels as he ran, screaming . . .

He awoke sweating, but the bull's bellowing was merely the gentle lowing of the dairy cows on their way to milking.

Now fully awake, he was aware of sweeter sounds of birdsong that filled his open window. Shaking free the web of nightmare, he washed and dressed for the day aware that the weather beyond the window looked promising.

He might as well make the most of this good fresh air before returning to the grime of Edinburgh's smoke-laden High Street and the Central Office of the City Police.

Concluding that dreams were contrary things signifying nothing, he tackled with promptitude the hearty breakfast set before him and contemplated Vince's imminent arrival.

Not for his stepson the train to Belford and an undignified scramble for the only hiring carriage. Vince would arrive in style in the comfort of the Gilchrists' own carriage, since their family coachbuilding business had accommodated Midlothian's gentry for two generations.

In a decidedly cheerful frame of mind, Faro checked with Bowden that there was a vacant bedroom should Dr Vincent Laurie require it. Then he set off into the village in search of Sergeant Yarrow and a vague hope of buying a suitable birthday gift for the twins' great-aunt Gilchrist.

He had noted that the local shop, in addition to supplying everything from food to farming implements, also displayed in its window pretty lace caps with ribbon streamers, a fashion the Queen had initiated and that widows and old ladies everywhere had eagerly adopted.

He was hesitating, undecided over the merits of a bewildering selection, when a voice at his elbow said: 'The one with more lace and less streamers, if it's for your mother. Sure, she'll like that, now.'

The Irish accent, the smiling face, was that of Imogen Crowe.

As he mumbled his thanks and handed the cap to the shopkeeper, she said: 'You'll not regret it. That's the one I'd have bought for my own mother. She'll be pleased too that it's good value. The rest are somewhat expensive,' she added in a whisper. 'And they won't launder as well.'

'I'm most grateful to you . . .'

But, turning, he saw she had paid for her own purchases, which looked like a bag of groceries, and was leaving the shop.

What miracle had caused such a change of heart in this

chilly lady, he wondered as, with his purchase pocketed, it remained only to hand over his notes to Sergeant Yarrow.

The station door was locked and bore a well-worn notice that anyone in need of the police should apply across the road. A printed hand helpfully pointed in the direction of the Dewars' cottage.

The door was opened very promptly. Mrs Dewar beamed on him. 'Do come in, sir.'

As he followed her into the kitchen, she said: 'Sandy isn't here at the moment, but I have a visitor I'm sure you'd like to meet.'

Seeing Imogen Crowe seated at the table, Faro hesitated. 'I don't wish to disturb you.'

'Not at all, not at all. Miss Crowe came for a recipe and we're just having a cup of tea. Perhaps you'll join us.'

Despite their recent encounter, amiable as it was, Miss Crowe was the last person Faro wished to see at that moment, and in this setting. He felt his dismay was shared by Miss Crowe, since the glint in Mrs Dewar's eye as she looked from one to the other with considerable sly satisfaction unmistakably proclaimed the matchmaker at work.

Faro remained standing, while he and Miss Crowe eyed each other warily. Yes, they said, they had met before. A bow from him, a sharp nod from her.

'Sandy went up the road in the pony cart. Sergeant Yarrow's still abed.' Mrs Dewar raised her eyes in the direction of the ceiling. 'He was late in last night. It's his morning off and I always take his breakfast up and put it outside his door,' she added reverently. 'A gentleman like him needs a bit of spoiling.

'If you take a walk up the road to the hillfort you'll meet Sandy on the way back. Perhaps you'd like to come to supper – ' she darted a look at Miss Crowe's glum face, 'both of you – on Sunday evening. I do a nice beef roast, too big for us now that our lads are away.'

Miss Crowe frowned, shook her head, glancing at Faro. He smiled and said: 'You are very kind, but my stepson is arriving this afternoon and I shall be leaving Elrigg.'

'You are leaving us – so soon.' Mrs Dewar darted an anxious look at Miss Crowe. 'That is such a pity. We are just getting to know you, isn't that so, miss?'

Her beaming smile in that lady's direction was rewarded by a polite but chilly inclination of the head enough to convince anyone less determined than Mrs Dewar that her romantic intentions were doomed to dismal failure.

'I'm sorry you must go, sir. I am sure you and this young lady would find much in common . . .'

Faro avoided Miss Crowe's eyes as he took his departure with more haste than good manners dictated, Mrs Dewar's well-meaning compliments soaring after him.

He had been through this ritual so many times, with so many mothers with daughters.

As he walked briskly up the road, he was a little astonished that a man past forty should still be a potential victim of the matchmaker's art. Would it never end, he thought? Would they never give up and accept him for what he was, a widower with growing daughters?

Having decided to put his notes into Yarrow's hands personally, he planned to enjoy the end of his stay in Elrigg with a pleasant stroll on a warm sunny morning. As he walked happily up the road whistling under his breath, he mentally shed 'Mr Faro: Insurance Investigator' and returned to his own identity.

He decided this would be a good opportunity to take another look at the hillfort on the excuse that Vince would want to know all about it. He had another stronger reason: to meet Hector Elrigg once more.

As he reached the pastureland, with the hillfort in sight, his nightmare returned and he approached with extreme caution.

No wild bulls roared down on him, the cattle were grazing nearer to the road than on his last visit, but still safely enclosed behind a sturdy-looking fence.

There was no sign of Hector Elrigg at the excavations

and having come this far Faro decided to try his cottage. There was no response but, finding the door partially open, he gazed inside. A fire glowed, the table was set for a perfunctory meal. The atmosphere was elegant, chairs and tables that would have been equally at home in the Castle; furnishings more opulent than he would have expected from a bachelor archaeologist's estate cottage.

He closed the door, thinking that Hector's good taste would not have gone amiss in Elrigg.

Hurrying back across the pastureland he was sure that the cattle had moved still nearer.

Although they appeared to be peacefully grazing he also observed that once again all faces had turned in his direction. They were watching him with unnerving stillness and intensity. Quickening his footsteps and resisting the almost unconquerable urge to run, he was thankful to bypass the hillfort and reach the safety of the road.

From beyond the fence, he looked at them in wonder. So little was left of early man's presence, but these beasts, who should rightly have been extinct long ago, continued to thrive, their survival dictated by some secret knowledge of the universe and obedience to the natural laws obliterated by layer upon layer of man's sophistication down the ages.

On the hilltop with the sun behind them, the standing stones looked more than ever like five headless women. What was their secret older than recorded time, what long forgotten rituals linked them with the hillfort and the wild cattle?

Intrigued by that insoluble mystery and having come this far on a fruitless errand, Faro decided to inspect them more carefully than the advent of the tiresome Miss Crowe had made possible.

Clambering along the margins of the farmer's field with its newly sown crops, he reached the summit of the circle, once more captivated by the views from this vantage point across two countries.

Taking a seat on a large stone, he looked down towards the now distant road. The outlines of the prehistoric fort were more clearly visible from this height, the sunlight casting shadows on the contours which had once sheltered the earliest inhabitants of Elrigg, the nomads who had settled here and given this place its first history.

There was a newer race of nomads now. And he saw a line of brightly coloured caravans trotting down the road, the sound of the horses, the tinkling of the pots and pans, dogs barking and children shouting, echoed through the air. A cheerful sound of bustling humanity, though he doubted whether the gypsies' return would be any more welcome here than it was on the meadows around Edinburgh.

They made careful circuit of the forbidden and dangerous pastureland and headed towards the riverbank where they would make temporary camp.

Far beyond the road twisting away below him, smoke rose into the still air indicating the village of Elrigg, an oasis nestling peacefully among undulating hills, lost in a fold of this wild barbaric land with its bloodsoaked history. Beyond the parkland the Castle's towers rose through the trees which hid the drive and the lodge gates.

Shading his eyes, he caught a glimpse of Miss Halliday's cottage and wondered if the twenty-year-old Walter Scott had also been intrigued by the riddle of Elrigg as he walked these roads and touched these stones. It pleased Faro to think that, with his famous novels still in the future, perhaps young Scott had conceived his love of the Borders which was to inspire *Marmion* and *The Bride of Lammermoor* in the Hallidays' farmhouse.

From the distant church he heard the sound of bells. Eleven o'clock, and reluctantly he made his way back downhill and, heading in the direction of the inn, he indulged in the pleasant fancy that on this very spot, echoing with his own footsteps, his hero had found inspiration or, in the years of his fame, wrestled with some particularly difficult passage of prose . . .

'Hey – mister . . .'

His reverie was interrupted by two young lads who erupted from the field and ran towards him waving their fishing rods.

'Mister, mister. Come quick!'

'Old Duffy's lying with his face in the burn . . .'

Chapter 20

Faro sprang over the fence and followed the two lads down the slope to swift-flowing water.

Half hidden by the overgrowing banks, Duffy lay motionless.

'He looks bad, doesn't he, mister?'

He did. Turning Duffy over, Faro said to the younger of the two who had the look of brothers: 'Go and keep a sharp look out for Constable Dewar. He's on the road somewhere. Send him over.' And to the other: 'Run and get Sergeant Yarrow. Fast as you can.'

'Will he be all right, mister?'

'I don't know.'

'Shall I get my father, sir? He's the vicar.'

'Yes, tell him. But get the Sergeant first.'

Obviously the Cairncross lad recognized the signs of death. And, left alone, Faro knew Duffy was dead. Drowned.

The signs were unmistakable, as was the smell of whisky about him.

Faro knelt by the body. Only another unfortunate accident, to be dismissed as one more coincidence, he told himself. And no connection with any information that, according to Bowden, Duffy had been anxious to impart (or sell) to the 'insurance mannie'.

Of course it was an accident, Yarrow and Dewar would say reassuringly. They knew Duffy well, the kind of man he was. Everyone had been expecting something like this. He drank too much, one day he'd keel over, fall into the river.

As Faro looked down at him, he noticed that from one clenched hand a thread hung. As he tugged, what at first glance was a silver coin rolled on the ground.

Faro picked it up, turned it over. If this meant what he thought it did, then Duffy's death was no accident. He had been murdered.

He was still thinking about the implications of his discovery when a horse and rider came into view. It was Yarrow, shortly followed by Dewar, the vicar, his sons and a couple of estate workers.

Reverend Cairncross knelt by the body, took the cold hands in his and murmured a prayer.

Almost roughly, Yarrow pushed him aside and also bent over the body. 'You can smell the drink on him.'

Faro leaned over and sniffed. 'You can that, Sergeant.'

'As if it had been poured over him,' sighed the vicar.

Yarrow gave him a sharp look, asked: 'Has he been moved?'

Faro indicated the Cairncross brothers. 'They found him. While they went for help, naturally I examined him to see if there were any signs of life.'

'Naturally,' echoed Yarrow sourly and turned to Dewar who was ready with the stretcher carried in the pony cart for emergencies, its use seldom required apart from farming accidents.

Reverend Cairncross said: 'I can do nothing here.'

'Has he any family?' Faro asked.

Yarrow answered, 'Not in these parts. There's a woman looks after his cottage.' And to Dewar, 'Best take him there till we make the proper arrangements. I'll walk back with Mr Faro.'

It wasn't a great distance, but Yarrow was slow on his feet and insisted on leading his horse. Faro's silence (related to whether this was an opportune moment to hand over the notes in his pocket) was presumed by Yarrow to be the layman's first sight of a drowned man or a corpse.

'You get very used to it in time,' he said sympathetically.

130

Faro could think of no suitable reply and Yarrow continued: 'Are you to be staying long in Elrigg?'

'Not much longer. My investigations are complete and my stepson is arriving today. We will probably take a few days' holiday before returning to Edinburgh.'

'That is awkward.'

Faro was conscious of Yarrow's intense gaze. 'Indeed?'

Yarrow cleared his throat apologetically. 'I might have to call on you to give evidence as you were the first on the scene, the first to touch the body. A passerby, of course, nothing to worry about,' he added hastily as if Faro's silence was an indication of guilt.

'I hope it won't take too long.'

Yarrow shook his head. 'Just routine, Mr Faro. Paperwork, that's all.' In a voice elaborately casual, he added, 'When did you last see Duffy alive, by the way?'

'A couple of days ago.'

'Oh! I thought you had a meeting arranged with him last night. At the inn. Heard Bowden discussing it with you.'

'True. But he failed to appear. As you know,' he reminded him gently.

Yarrow considered that for a moment, nodded. 'Have you any idea what it was he wanted to talk to you about?'

'None at all.'

'You've talked to him before? Privately, I mean.'

'Never. Bowden suggested that he probably wanted to borrow money.'

There was a slight pause. 'Can you think of any reason why he should imagine that a stranger to the district would be willing to give him money?'

'I haven't the least idea, Sergeant.'

Yarrow stared ahead, frowning. 'May I ask your whereabouts yesterday evening?'

'Certainly. I was at the inn. As you know.' Faro's laugh held a note of exasperation. What was Yarrow getting at?

Yarrow did not share his amusement. He continued to eye him sternly. 'You were seen in the vicinity near where Duffy was found.'

131

'I might well have been. I had an evening stroll.' And Faro turned to him, his laughter now disbelieving. He was being cross-examined. Detective Inspector Faro was a suspect.

His mirth faded at Yarrow's expression.

'It was the earlier part of the evening I was considering – before we met.'

'Oh, I have an alibi for that too, if that's what you're asking, I was visiting Miss Halliday. She will vouch for me. We had tea together and she was most informative on the history of the village – and her clever pupils. We talked about Sir Walter Scott and I admired some of her paintings. She's very good.'

Yarrow nodded. 'So I've heard. Could have made a name for herself.'

Relieved at this change of subject and return to normal conversation, Faro said: 'That I can believe. There was one portrait – of a young lad, one of her pupils, a brilliant lad by all accounts – killed in a shooting accident. He looked ready to speak – it was remarkably lifelike . . .'

Yarrow frowned. 'That would be one of the beaters. They still talk about him. Before my time, but memories are long in places like this.' As they approached the inn, he added: 'Thank you for your help, Mr Faro. Perhaps you'll let me know when you're leaving in case I need to talk to you again.'

Faro watched him go. Yarrow obviously suspected that Duffy's death might not have been an accident. Having overheard the poacher asking for Faro at the inn was enough to alert any policeman worthy of the name of detective when a man is subsequently found dead.

Faro was not quite as amused as he might have been to find himself in the classic situation of the stranger, the newcomer to the district, immediately under suspicion and the first to be questioned.

As he awaited Vince's arrival, he thought about the tiny piece of evidence resting in his pocket beside his notes on the two deaths at Elrigg. As he wrestled with his conscience he decided that Duffy's death could not have come at a worse time. Another twenty-four hours and he would have been clear of Elrigg.

Clear of suspicion!

Chapter 21

'You could tell Yarrow who you are, of course,' said Vince as he unpacked and hung an array of shirts and cravats in the capacious wardrobe. He sounded irritable and with good reason.

Within their first few moments of conversation on his arrival at the inn, he had seen fast disappearing all hopes of that splendid walking holiday he was looking forward to. His stepfather had got himself hopelessly involved in yet another crime.

'You're impossible, Stepfather, too conscientious by far. These murders, if murders they are, have nothing to do with you. This isn't your province. You know that perfectly well. The Northumberland Constabulary will tell you sharp enough that you are out of order, Inspector Faro.'

He shrugged. "And as for this latest happening, it isn't unknown for a poacher who's fond of the drink to accidentally drown while under the influence.'

'Perhaps you're right, Vince,' said Faro weakly, almost eager to be persuaded.

'Of course I am.' Vince closed the wardrobe door, thrust his valise under the bed and said: 'Let's join the others.' He led the way downstairs to where Owen and Olivia were already enjoying afternoon tea in front of a large fire.

'Two more places, Mr Bowden, if you please,' said Faro.

Approaching the Gilchrists, he saw that an adjoining side table was solely occupied by Imogen Crowe, awaiting her order.

She looked up and smiled a friendly greeting.

Faro, somewhat taken aback, suspected that the recipient of this transformed Miss Crowe was his handsome stepson. Vince, with his fair curls, his deceptively angelic countenance, had that effect upon young women.

'Two places, did you say, sir?' said Bowden.

Olivia looked at Faro, smiled encouragingly and said quite loudly, 'Why don't you ask your friend to join us, sir?'

'Heavens, no.' whispered Faro, assiduously turning his back on Miss Crowe.

Olivia considered that lady for a moment and gave him a reproachful look. 'A pity to have her sitting on her own, is it not?' she murmured.

'Yes, indeed,' responded her brother with an admiring glance at Miss Crowe. 'The more the merrier, I always say.'

Vince turned, joined in his friend's enthusiasm, bowed in her direction and was rewarded by even more smiling Irish eyes, a pretty inclination of dark red curls.

Turning sharply to Faro he said enthusiastically, 'Yes, Stepfather, why not?'

'No,' said Faro firmly, almost too loudly for politeness. While he studied his empty plate with tightly closed lips, the others looked across at Miss Crowe, were pleased by what they saw and stared back at Faro encouragingly.

Their expressions made him angry. Mrs Dewar's weakness it seemed was shared not only by most womankind, but had spread to his own family and friends.

Matchmaking. He grimaced, he was sick and tired of it. He had thought Olivia Gilchrist might have more sense.

But as the tea was poured and the scones eaten at a leisurely pace, Miss Crowe was forgotten. Out of the corner of his eye Faro thankfully watched her depart. Grateful that the jarring incident created by her presence was over, he joined in the laughter as the two young men reminisced about college days, meanwhile keeping a sharp eye on Olivia's reaction to his stepson.

He would have been shocked indeed had someone told him that he was indulging in exactly the same behaviour as poor Mrs Dewar and that this pairing off was endemic in the human race.

The young couple seemed so fond of each other, laughing, teasing. Almost like brother and sister. He groaned. That was what he feared, that they had been dear friends too long for romance to blossom.

'Delightful place, this, sir,' said Owen. 'You were lucky to find it. Full of atmosphere.'

'It wasn't difficult to find,' Faro laughed. 'It's the only place.'

'My bedroom floor squeaks abominably,' said Vince.

'Quite right,' said Olivia solemnly. 'That will keep you from straying.' Then to Faro: 'Great-Aunt is so sorry she couldn't accommodate Vince too. Her cottage is just too tiny. Have you told your stepfather the arrangements, Vince?'

'I haven't. We've had other matters to discuss.'

'Nothing as important as the party.' And leaning over she said: 'You mean he hasn't told you that we have been invited to the Castle here for Great-Aunt's birthday celebration?'

When Faro shook his head, she looked at Vince.

'Dash it all, Olivia. I've been keeping it a secret – a surprise, as you told me,' was the reproachful response.

'Honestly – men!' Olivia gave a despairing sigh and turned to her brother. 'You tell him, Owen. This is so exciting – you being here already, sir,' she added to Faro.

'Hold on, Livvy,' said Owen. 'We've just heard ourselves, when we called in to see Great-Aunt. She was governess to Mark Elrigg long ago. They have always been very close. When Mark's mother died, he didn't even as a child get on very well with his stepfather – ' He looked at Vince and Faro. 'Not like some I could name. Anyway, he turned to Great-Aunt for love and comfort. He's never forgotten her kindness and he's kept in touch with her by letter and frequent visits to Branxton.'

'The really exciting part is that we've been asked to stay the night at the Castle after the party, I'm so looking forward to that,' Olivia put in. 'Apparently Mark wouldn't hear of his dear Miss Gilchrist travelling all that way back home.'

'Great-Aunt says he has a very special surprise for her . . .'

Anything concerning the Elriggs was of great interest and this indeed might prove a rewarding turn of events, thought Faro. As Vince's glum expression expressed a certain lack of enthusiasm, he realized that any change of plans, or possible new evidence of mayhem at the Castle, upset his own wishes to get Faro away from Elrigg as speedily as possible.

At that moment, however, Faro's chief concern was how he could escape the embarrassing situation whereby his real identity would have to be revealed and explained to Mark and Lady Elrigg.

Suddenly he became aware of a figure hovering behind him.

'Excuse me, sir.'

It was Dewar. 'Could I have a word, sir?'

As the constable strode purposefully in the direction of the bar, Faro followed him with a sinking sense of disaster. Long ago he had realized the truth of the maxim that murders, like troubles, seldom come singly.

He was not to be disappointed.

'Miss Halliday's cottage has been broken into, sir. She's been badly hurt. Sergeant Yarrow found her lying at the bottom of the staircase when he went to collect his quarantine papers for the authorities. He reckons she probably disturbed the burglar.'

'Have you any idea who . . .?'

Dewar shrugged. 'Sergeant reckons it might have been Duffy.'

'Duffy? But how could—'

'Well, Dr Brand says it might have happened late last night, before his accident.' Dewar shook his head. 'I don't agree, sir. Duffy was ready to lift anything that ain't nailed down, but I've never known him resort to breaking and entering.'

'Was there a motive?' Faro asked.

'What kind of motive would that be, sir?'

'Did she have anything of value?' Faro said impatiently, remembering a few nice pieces of furniture, antiques but hardly things with an immediate resale value for a poacher. 'And how did he get in?'

Dewar looked astonished at this remark. 'Bless you, sir, no one round here ever locks their doors. We don't live in that kind of society. We all trust one another.'

In Miss Halliday's case badly misplaced, thought Faro, as Dewar's naïvety confirmed his original assessment that the constable's reaction to real crime would be shocked disbelief. Such things were unthinkable in Elrigg.

'Where is Miss Halliday now?'

'Dr Brand says she's concussed, got a nasty shock, that's for sure. The minister's wife will look after her till she's better. We're a caring society, here, sir,' he added defensively in case Faro should be in any danger of thinking otherwise.

He had indeed read Faro's thoughts. Very caring indeed, especially when some person hit her on the head and left her for dead.

'Did she have any difficult pupils?' he asked.

Dewar's eyes widened in horror at such implication.

'I get your drift, sir. But you're wrong. The children are all obedient and law abiding, sir. Things might be diffferent in big cities like where you come from,' he added stiffly. 'But here the bairns are brought up from their earliest days to be God-fearing and to respect their parents and other people. Besides Miss Halliday's loved by everyone, she's taught several decades their three Rs. Now if you'll excuse me, sir.'

With an air of silent reprimand, Dewar saluted him gravely and marched out of the inn.

At the table he had just left, the twins were preparing to

138

return to Branxton. Waving them off, the air heavy with instructions for the following day's festivities, Vince smiled:

'Well, that's that. What shall we do now?'

'A walk, perhaps.'

'A good idea. What did your local constable want?'

Faro told him about Miss Halliday and the break-in.

Vince, adept at reading his stepfather's mind, sighed deeply. 'So that's where we're going?'

Faro nodded eagerly. 'Bearing in mind that doors are never locked in this law-abiding community I thought we might avail ourselves of a little private investigation.'

Vince's sigh was despairing this time. 'You never give up, do you, Stepfather?'

'She was very kind to me. I owe her that much. And I'm very curious. I'd like you to see her paintings too. They're very impressive.'

'How far is it?' Vince demanded, in a voice notable for a lack of enthusiasm, Faro having temporarily overlooked the fact that his stepson felt the same way about amateur painters as he did about amateur thespians.

'We'll do it in forty minutes, there and back,' he said encouragingly.

Vince thought about it and yawned. 'Forgive me, Stepfather, if I don't come with you. Truth is, I'm devilish tired. Out till the wee sma' hours delivering a baby.'

Faro smiled sympathetically. 'I've noticed that they always seem to choose times when it's least convenient for your social life.'

Vince nodded, stretching his arms above his head. 'Must be on form for the long day tomorrow. I think, if you'll excuse me, I'll take a bath. Bowden assures me hip baths are readily available. He even has a special room put aside for such ablutions. See you at dinner, eh?'

Setting off for Miss Halliday's cottage alone, Faro felt a little lonely, his spirits cast down. When he got too close to a case and became enmeshed and thoroughly baffled, it was almost always Vince who could be relied upon to stand back and view it coolly from a different and often enlightened angle.

If only Vince had been free of other obligations this time. He shouldn't really feel like this, he told himself sternly, he had guessed that his stepson would not be a great deal of use on this occasion, involved with the Gilchrists and their great-aunt's birthday celebrations.

He sighed. The sooner he got used to the new regime, the better for everyone. It was what he had always wanted for Vince, to see him happy with a girl like Olivia. What he was experiencing, this sudden bitter shaft of loneliness, was no more than the normal pattern of parenthood, a glimpse into the future when he would no longer enjoy the comradeship they had shared since Vince's boyhood.

Opening the door of Miss Halliday's cottage cautiously, he noted that it was remarkably tidy inside. In the kitchen, a few papers lay scattered on the floor, a broken ornament, a shattered cup, but there was a gold watch on the sideboard and a purse full of sovereigns.

Money had not been the burglar's object.

Turning back again to the kitchen table, he noticed that it was set for two people, one each side of the table; one cup was almost full, the other empty.

He stood back and regarded the scene carefully. The clues were all here.

Miss Halliday had been attacked by someone she knew well enough to take out her best china. He looked at the mantelpiece and visualized the scene indicated by two broken ornaments and a framed photograph on the floor, swept off by her arm no doubt as she fought off her attacker.

Picking them up and returning them to their rightful places with the complete recall that was one of his remarkable assets, he saw that Sir Walter Scott's framed letter was missing. Walking round the table again, he stood beside the cup of tea that had been abandoned. Opposite it, the painting of the boy Eric was missing.

As he closed the door, he had no longer the least doubt that the killer of Sir Archie and the poacher Duffy had also attacked Miss Halliday. His experience indicated that the three people were linked in a murderous chain of events.

Or could it be that the presence of Detective Inspector Faro upset someone with a guilty conscience?

Going over his conversation with Miss Halliday, he decided to cross the road to the Castle lodge and call upon Miss Imogen Crowe.

There was no response and trying the door he found it unlocked. He was not as surprised as he should have been to see Scott's letter lying on her kitchen table.

He picked it up. His fascinated re-reading of it was interrupted by Miss Crowe's arrival.

Then she saw what he held and pointed an accusing finger.

'No!' He forestalled her accusation with one of his own. 'This is, I believe, the property of Miss Halliday.'

'It is. She lent it to me. To make a copy.'

Faro laughed. 'Oh, did she indeed? And do you know where she is at this moment?'

Miss Crowe shrugged. 'Across the road in her house, I expect.'

Faro leaned on the table. 'Then you expect wrong, miss. Someone broke into her house last night. She was attacked—'

There was a shocked exclamation as Miss Crowe asked: 'Is she all right?'

'She is unconscious.'

'Where is she? I'll look after her—'

'No need to trouble yourself, the minister's wife is more than capable.'

Miss Crowe clenched her hands. 'Will she recover?'

'Who knows?'

'But how did it happen – I mean—'

'We gather she intercepted a burglar.'

141

'A burglar?' whispered Imogen Crowe.

'That is so, miss.' And, laying down the letter, he tapped its frame. 'I suppose you know you could go to gaol for that.'

He had the dubious satisfaction of seeing her face turn deathly pale, white as the cloth on the kitchen table, as he turned on his heel and left her.

Chapter 22

At the inn, Faro found Vince looking forward eagerly to supper. Refreshed and bathed, in a good humour, he was eager to listen to his stepfather's latest experiences.

'You had better get it all off your chest,' he said, 'then you can consider the case finally closed and we can begin to enjoy ourselves.'

'First of all, there's this visit to the Castle. They don't know I'm a detective and it's bound to come out.'

'Ah, I'm well ahead of you there. I've explained to the twins and to Miss Gilchrist that you are on a secret mission of national importance. They were very impressed and you can rely on them not to give the game away. Now, what have you found out?'

As Faro went through the details, item by item, Vince listened carefully: 'One thing is obvious, those missing paintings are tucked safely away somewhere in the attics of the Castle. To be brought out and discreetly restored to the original places, once Her Majesty has forgotten all about them. I think it will be safe enough for I doubt whether Bertie will make any more incognito visits to Elrigg, don't you agree?'

'Indeed. Two unfortunate fatal accidents should be enough to cool even his ardour,' said Faro.

'And you can certainly remove from your mind that he had any part in this bull's horn business. That is hardly his style. I understand he is not even passable with a rifle.' Vince paused to take a second helping of game pie. 'I'd hazard a guess that Philip Gray's death was an accident.

As for the laird's – that comes into the dubious area of "might-have-been-murder". Trouble was you arrived far too late to be of any use proving anything to the contrary.'

'True enough, even if they had wanted my help,' said Faro. 'With the blessing of Sergeant Yarrow and the Northumberland Constabulary, the trail was cold.'

'Worse than that, Stepfather. As far as I can see there isn't a shred of real evidence against anyone. As for your suspects. Well, I'd be prepared to bet a great deal of money that it wasn't Lady Elrigg in the classic role of husband-murderer. I'm sure she had enough experience of the wicked world not to get rid of the goose that was laying the golden eggs for her.

'As for Mark. I'll tell you more when I meet him, but I'd be surprised because it doesn't sound likely, from what I've heard of him through the Gilchrists. And from what you've told me, there is no real evidence of guilty lovers.'

Vince gestured with his fork. 'I wonder why there are no children to the Elrigg marriage. As a doctor that intrigues me most. Not only the first marriage to Mark's mother, which proves she could bear children, but what about the second to this nubile young woman? Could it be, do you think, that Sir Archie was impotent? That he knew it and that's why he was prepared, even eager, to make his stepson, who had a dash of the genuine Elrigg blood, his heir?'

'You could be right, Vince lad. That possibility had never occurred to me, and it's certainly an interesting one. Explains a lot of things.'

'Who else have we?' Vince looked down at Faro's notes lying beside his plate. 'You do this uncommonly well, Stepfather. You are to be congratulated on a masterpiece of clarity. Sergeant Yarrow will be grateful, I'm sure. Let's see . . .

'Hector Elrigg, the disgruntled archaeologist who believes that he was cheated out of his inheritance by a reprobate father. He would be my best bet, he has the most impressive motive, a wound festering over the years.

144

I realize you haven't much in the way of evidence, but still – there may be something important we've missed.'

As Vince flicked back through the notes, Faro shook his head. 'You may be right, yet I have a feeling – no more than that – just a feeling that we're dealing with the dedicated historian who is keener on getting on with his work, digging the hillfort and the standing stones than being laird of Elrigg.'

'Meanwhile, of course,' said Vince, 'we may have a number of dissatisfied tenants whose activities as well as their names are unknown to you, since there has been neither time nor opportunity to conduct a thorough investigation. I appreciate that distances to be travelled single-handed are somewhat daunting.'

And rubbing his chin thoughtfully, 'What about the good Dr Brand whose daughter drowned in the ornamental lake? If she was seduced by the laird, he would have good reason for killing him off.'

'But since you've suggested the impotence factor, the pregnancy fits in with the lover who was sent away in disgrace.'

'True,' said Vince. 'Then who are we left with? The unfortunate poacher, Duffy.'

'No, but I do think he knew something, or had seen something.'

'Perhaps he gossiped and was overheard?'

Faro agreed. 'Not a man of discreet habits, I gather from Bowden. Blackmail would be a profitable business for him.'

Vince consulted the list again. 'I think we can safely cross off the Reverend Cairncross in spite of his daughter's odd reaction to the Elriggs. And, as a victim, Miss Halliday.'

'I can't see any reason why she would want to murder Sir Archie,' said Faro.

'But there's always Miss Imogen Crowe and your latest foray into a different sort of crime. What was her motive for stealing the portrait?'

'It wasn't the portrait, Vince. It was Sir Walter Scott's letter.' Faro frowned. 'I keep going over that scene in Miss Halliday's kitchen. There's something there, if only I could remember. Something I saw.'

'It'll come, I'm sure,' said Vince soothingly. 'The only link I can see is that she is Irish and so was Philip Gray. But that's a bit tenuous.'

Vince was aware that he no longer had his stepfather's attention. 'What's wrong?'

Faro shook his head. 'Just an idea I've had.'

He was silent so long that Vince laid aside the papers and said: 'By the way, the carriage is coming for us in the morning. There's to be a Maytime pageant at Branxton, with a celebration of Miss Gilchrist's birthday among other things. There'll be floats, so I'm told, with the children performing scenes from history, a monologue written about the Battle of Flodden. What do you think, Stepfather?'

'Think?' Faro came back to him with a start. 'I don't know,' he said lamely. 'What was it you were saying?'

Patiently Vince repeated the programme of the day's activities and Faro shook his head very firmly. 'No, Vince lad. Absolutely not. I'll save my energies for the festivities at the Castle. I just might have to have my wits about me then.'

Vince considered him. 'Anything you'd like to share, Stepfather? Some new observations?'

Faro smiled. 'Only when I can give them substance and that may take some time.'

Next morning, having seen Vince off, Faro was deciding how he could most profitably spend his day when Sergeant Yarrow arrived at the inn. After a perfunctory greeting he saluted Faro gravely and said: 'Sir, I owe you an apology.'

Faro smiled vaguely. 'Ah, you have decided to remove me from your list of suspects?'

Yarrow looked contrite. 'Dewar has just told me who you are, sir. I cannot tell you—'

'Think nothing of it, Sergeant. It's the sort of mistake any policeman worth his salt might make. You are to be commended for that.'

Yarrow smiled wryly. 'It's the lesson we all learn, isn't it? First on the scene most often is the prime suspect.'

'And a stranger in the neighbourhood, too,' said Faro.

Yarrow held out his hand. 'May I take this opportunity of welcoming your assistance, sir. Anything at all you may have observed during your time here might be of considerable help to us.'

When Faro didn't reply immediately, Yarrow continued to regard him quizzically. 'You think Sir Archie was murdered? Political, maybe. Equerry to the Prince of Wales and that sort of thing?'

Faro remained silent, and Yarrow shrugged. 'Come now, sir, that is obviously the real reason why you are here. We do know something of your background—'

'Not in this instance, Sergeant. Such matters – crimes or political investigations, if you wish – in Elrigg are entirely the province of the Northumberland Constabulary or the Metropolitan Police, you know that. And Edinburgh City Police would have no right to interfere.'

Yarrow's eyebrows raised mockingly. 'I can hardly believe that a man as important as yourself would have been sent down here to investigate some missing paintings.'

'You must take my word for that. Let us say I was here on behalf of a very important client. That is all I can tell you, I'm afraid.'

Sergeant Yarrow looked thoughtful. 'I wonder if you have any ideas about Miss Halliday's attacker.'

'None at all. Living here you must know a great deal more than any stranger about likely suspects.'

'True. There aren't many, I can assure you. Take the man Duffy, he's the nearest we get to criminal activities, he's well known as a petty thief, but we have never been able to pin anything big on him, he was too wily for that.'

Faro remembered Dewar's words. 'You think he might have attacked Miss Halliday first – before his accident?'

Yarrow nodded eagerly. 'I'm positive that's the way of it. Miss Halliday's home-made wine was famous. He couldn't resist drink of any kind. Might have sampled a bottle with dire effects. She caught him at it – and we know the rest.'

Faro looked at him. There had been no evidence of empty bottles or glasses in that disturbed room. 'You are seriously considering this theory?'

'Except that we have no record of Duffy ever being violent, or of breaking and entering a private residence. A genial rogue rather than a genuine criminal.'

'What about the gypsies? Have you considered that there might be less genial rogues among them and that their arrival coincided with Miss Halliday's attack and Duffy's death?'

Yarrow shook his head. 'Assault and battery isn't their style at all. Like Duffy, it's more clothes off lines and a hen or two.' After a long pause, he added: 'There is, however, one matter which is perturbing me greatly at the moment. A matter that is well out of our province, but perhaps with your greater experience you could advise me.'

'If I can.'

Again Yarrow hesitated before continuing: 'It concerns the woman Imogen Crowe. Did you know, by any chance, that she has a police record?'

Faro shook his head. This was a surprise – or was it?

'What did she do?'

'Went to gaol for harbouring Fenian terrorists. I've been keeping an eye on Miss Crowe's activities. I don't suppose you remember the case in Scotland. There was a Brendan Crowe – her uncle and guardian, so she claimed – who took a shot at the Queen riding in St James's Park.'

Faro sighed. 'I vaguely remember the case. There have been similar incidents. About twelve years ago, wasn't it?'

Yarrow regarded him admiringly. 'Correct first time, sir. Year after the Prince Consort died and Her Majesty had gained a great deal of public support and sympathy, her being a widow and so forth. Crowe was shot and wounded

148

by us – we cornered him but he managed to escape to his lodgings. Topped himself before he could be arrested—'

'And his niece – Miss Crowe?'

'She was in the house with him, fought the arresting officers tooth and nail. Protested that she knew nothing about his political activities. We didn't believe a word of it, naturally, so she was sentenced as accessory. Lucky for her that he never stood trial or she might have been hanged.'

'She must have been very young at the time,' said Faro.

'Not all that young, sir, eighteen. Old enough to know right from wrong, I'd say.'

It was a situation Faro knew well and one that he deplored. A public outcry means that the police are expected to produce a scapegoat, someone the mob could vent their anger on. An eighteen-year-old girl, terrified and confused, horrified by her guardian's death, would do excellently.

'She was very probably speaking the truth,' he said.

'Once a terrorist, always a terrorist.' Yarrow gave him a hard look. Clearly, he did not share Faro's sentiments. 'An eye for an eye, a tooth for a tooth,' he added grimly. 'The Bible got it right, you know.'

When Faro said nothing, Yarrow added: 'We put her behind bars for a couple of years.'

'What is she doing in Elrigg then?' asked Faro, already knowing the answer.

'She writes books.'

'Romances?'

Yarrow laughed. 'Hardly sir. About Women's Rights, the sort of thing females who have been in prison write if they are literate, encouraging other women to believe that they've been ill-treated – all that sort of nonsense. Shouldn't be allowed.'

Faro felt a fleeting compassion for Imogen Crowe, knowing only too well the notorious conditions of women's prisons in London: verminous, ill-treated prisoners, starved and beaten. Unthinkable that she might have been innocent, as she claimed.

Yarrow was regarding him shrewdly. 'When Dewar told me about you, my first thought was: is he here in connection with Imogen Crowe? And your very important client has confirmed that for me. You can rely on my discretion, of course, sir, and you don't need to say whether I'm right or wrong. I'll understand perfectly.'

When Faro smiled, he continued: 'I'd hazard a guess that authority believe, with the Prince of Wales being a frequent visitor to the Castle, that there might be a Fenian plot and that she's here to spy for them.'

As he waited for a reply, he scanned Faro's face carefully. 'You think she might be involved in something?'

This was a new aspect of the case which had never occurred to Faro. Could Yarrow be right? There had been no mention of Fenian activities. Surely the Prime Minister would have known and the Edinburgh City Police would have been alerted in the interests of national security even though it was outside their province.

He shook his head. 'It doesn't sound like a Fenian plot to me.'

Yarrow looked disappointed. 'That actor fellow. The one who was gored by one of the wild cattle. He was Irish too, been on the boards in Dublin. Food for thought, eh, sir?' said Yarrow.

'It is indeed.'

'I'm about to look in and see how Miss Halliday is. I don't suppose . . .'

'Yes, of course, I'll come with you.'

As they walked towards the Manse, in the light of Yarrow's information regarding Imogen Crowe, Faro decided to err on the side of caution and keep his observations – and his notes – to himself for the time being.

Chapter 23

Mrs Cairncross's relieved expression as she greeted them at the Manse said that their worst fears had not been realized.

'Yes, she's awake, the poor dear. Dr Brand's with her now.'

At that moment the doctor descended the stairs, smiling and shaking his head when he saw Yarrow. 'You won't be needed after all, Sergeant. No need to put cuffs on anyone this time. Simple explanation. Rattling window woke her up, she came down and tripped on the stairs in the dark. Tried to save herself, grabbed at the mantelpiece and hit her head a mighty crack on the hearth as she fell. Good job she's got a thick skull—'

'There was no burglar?' Yarrow sounded shocked.

'That's what she says,' said the doctor cheerfully, fastening his bag and turning to Mrs Cairncross. 'Told me to say, yes, please, ma'am, she would like her breakfast now.'

'Can we see her?' demanded Yarrow.

'Later. We must keep her quiet for a while.' And to the minister's wife, 'Keep her in bed for a day or two, if you can manage.'

'I'll do my best, Doctor, but she's a very determined lady.'

Dr Brand frowned, looking at the two men. 'I think I'd best be honest with you. I don't think our dear Miss Halliday is speaking the truth.'

'I knew it,' said Yarrow triumphantly. 'She's protecting someone, that's for sure.'

The doctor smiled. 'Only herself, Sergeant.'

'I don't understand.'

'You might if you were her age. She should have retired long ago but she's determined to keep on teaching until she drops – which, candidly, she will do quite soon if she doesn't give up. You see, the fall she took I believe was due to a mild heart attack.'

'A heart attack, oh, the poor dear,' said Mrs Cairncross. 'How on earth will she continue at the school?'

'I suspect the very same thought is troubling her, so she makes light of it, says it was only a bad fall. I've examined her and found no damage, no paralysis of arms and legs or facial muscles, so we can deduce that this was just a warning. A warning which she must take seriously. Like some of my other patients,' he added, darting a significant look at Yarrow. 'You haven't been to see me lately.'

'I'm much too busy to fuss about aches and pains. They've been with me a long time,' said Yarrow brusquely, leaving Faro to wonder if the greyness of his complexion was natural or due to some more serious cause, as Imogen Crowe had hinted.

'What about the school, Doctor?' asked Mrs Cairncross, remembering her brood of children and their future.

'She must get help, a younger woman, to take some of the burden—'

He was interrupted by Miss Halliday, calling from upstairs: 'Hell–o – Mrs Cairncross, are you there?'

Mrs Cairncross picked up the tray. 'She's out of bed. I knew it. Once my back was turned. Coming, my dear.'

'I'll be back when she's had her breakfast,' said Yarrow.

Dr Brand nodded. 'You come with me, Sergeant.'

When Yarrow protested with a helpless look at Faro, the doctor seized his arm firmly. 'I've got some of my splendid pills waiting for you.'

Faro lingered, waiting for Mrs Cairncross to return. 'Do you think I might have a few words with Miss Halliday? I'm to leave Elrigg shortly. This might be my last chance.'

Mrs Cairncross looked doubtful. 'If you think it will be all right, sir. You won't tire her, will you?'

Miss Halliday was sitting up in bed, her face badly bruised but otherwise she was remarkably cheerful. When he exclaimed sympathetically, she smiled painfully. 'I'm perfectly all right, no bones broken. A silly accident, but I'll be back with my children on Monday. It's good of you to come and say goodbye—'

'There is something else, Miss Halliday. I realize this is an inappropriate time – Sir Walter's letter. I was absolutely fascinated—'

'And you would like a copy. I don't have it, I'm afraid.' She laughed at his solemn expression. 'Ask Miss Crowe. She looked in after you yesterday and I lent it to her for that very reason.'

And Faro had the grace to feel ashamed.

Miss Molly Gilchrist's visit to Elrigg Castle was to be memorable for its surprises, none of which could have been anticipated by the guests.

The sunny warm weather held and the gardens, with their budding trees laden with birdsong, made a pretty and nostalgic background for the old lady, whose face was a map of her life, of its joys and sorrows. Her eyes, still bright, constantly searched for her beloved pupil, Mark.

'Where is he?' she whispered, as she perambulated the gardens on Faro's arm. 'Dear, dear, I did expect he would be here to greet his guests,' she added anxiously. 'And he did promise me a nice surprise. We share the same birthday, you know. He is twenty-five today,' she added proudly.

'A double celebration,' said Owen. 'No doubt that is what is keeping him.'

And Faro remembered that this was the day Mark came of age, when all of Elrigg would be his.

'These gardens must be full of memories for you,' said Olivia. 'Is it exciting to come back?'

'It is indeed.' And Miss Gilchrist proceeded to regale

them with stories of Mark's childhood. As is so often the case of rich children whose parents had little time for them, motherless Mark had been treated by her more as son than pupil. He had returned her devotion and had kept in touch with her over the years, by letter and by frequent visits.

Suddenly two figures emerged from the topiary surrounding the rose garden. Lady Elrigg walked swiftly towards them, apologizing for Mark's absence. This was greeted by an audible sigh of relief from Miss Gilchrist and, as introductions were made, Faro observed that Lady Elrigg's companion Miss Kent stepped back, as if eager for the shadows of the great cypress hedge. She curtsied to the group and then, in an almost imperceptible gesture, touched her mistress's arm.

Still smiling, Lady Elrigg turned to her immediately and together they moved a little distance away. Apparently the talk was brief but urgent, for with a quick glance towards the assembled guests, Miss Kent hurried off in the direction of the Castle.

'Some urgent domestic niceties I seem to have overlooked for this evening,' they were informed. 'Fortunately Miss Kent remembered.'

But Faro wasn't at all sure she was speaking the truth. Her colour had heightened slightly and he felt certain her sharp, uncertain glance had concerned the guests and something more important than was warranted by a housekeeping consultation.

'I trust your rooms are quite comfortable?' At the murmurs of 'Very' and 'Delightful', Lady Elrigg smiled. 'And now, if you will excuse me. We will meet again in the drawing room at five o'clock.'

'Will Mark be there?' Miss Gilchrist asked in a bewildered voice.

Lady Elrigg took her hands. 'Of course, my dear, of course, he will. Now do enjoy the last of the sunshine while you can.'

When they returned to the house, Mark rushed out to

greet them. Exchanging hugs and kisses with a relieved and tearful Miss Gilchrist, he said: 'I so much wanted you to be here, I have a very special surprise for you.'

It was a surprise for everyone. In the drawing room Poppy Elrigg now wore a gown of violet lace and the Elrigg diamonds. Even in humbler attire she would have overshadowed every other female present.

Hector Elrigg arrived with Dr Brand and both greeted the Elriggs with a geniality that raised Faro's eyebrows a little considering how vehemently they had both railed against Sir Archie. Presumably their angry feelings did not extend to his pretty widow and his stepson.

Faro made a mental note that Hector in particular had taken great pains with his appearance. His suit, although a little out of fashion, was considerably smarter than the rough countryman's attire he normally appeared in. Dr Brand too was wearing what Faro suspected was his Sunday best.

The latecomer was Imogen Crowe.

This was indeed a surprise and not a particularly pleasant one for Faro. He suspected he would be seated next to her at dinner. But much was to happen before that.

'Right,' said Mark. 'Now that everyone is here, will you please follow me.' He gave his ex-governess his arm and the group made their way back down the staircase out and across the courtyard to the private chapel which had served the Elriggs of several past generations.

With his hand on the open door, Mark put his arm about Miss Gilchrist. 'This dear lady, as you all know, has been my mother in every way but the accident of birth. She is the dearest in all the world to me – except for one person,' he smiled, 'and it is appropriate that she should stand by me on my wedding day.'

'Your wedding day!'

There was a very audible gasp from the group at this unexpected announcement. He said: 'Yes, dear friends, I am to be married.' And throwing open the door, he said, 'There is my bride.'

Standing before Reverend Cairncross at the altar were his wife and, now radiant in her bridal gown, their once weeping daughter Harriet, whom Faro had met briefly in the churchyard.

Turning to Molly Gilchrist, Mark said: 'I shall want your blessing.'

'That you have always had, my dearest boy. I am so happy for you.'

And so they were wed. Poppy Elrigg was obviously delighted and had relished helping Mark plan the event with such great secrecy. As for Faro, he was glad to have been in grave error regarding the affection of two young people drawn together in a trying household.

Reverend Cairncross and his wife were doubtless gratified by this conclusion to their own problem for, without wishing to be indelicate, or stare too heavily, it was obvious that Harriet was pregnant.

The wedding party returned jubilantly indoors to dine in the elegant room with its eighteenth-century damask wall-hangings, faded but still intact. The faces of ghostly bygone Elriggs stared down from the walls at the diners in a setting that was everything an old family servant like Miss Gilchrist could have wished for.

It was also an occasion to provide Faro with some interesting observations and conclusions.

'Miss Kent has asked to be excused,' said Poppy Elrigg. 'She suffers from wretched headaches and this one refuses to disappear.'

Vince offered pills, Aunt Molly offered reliable home remedies seconded very firmly by Imogen, while Olivia and her brother offered sympathy.

'I was hoping to see her again,' murmured Olivia to Vince and when he said 'Really', she put a hand to her lips, glancing at Faro, who had overheard.

'Shh – tell you later.'

As Faro had suspected, Imogen Crowe was seated next to him at table with Hector on her other side. However, with much good food and wine, particularly the latter, he found himself oddly forgiving and forgetful of her disagreeable qualities. They talked about books and Faro found her also knowledgeable about his own particular favourites, Shakespeare and Mr Dickens.

Quite remarkably so, he thought, and found himself looking at her and remembering what Yarrow had told him about her past. Miss Crowe having survived a gaol sentence and writing books about it would never have been tolerated at most Edinburgh dinner tables. In the society he knew there, she would be shunned, a social outcast.

There was one more event to be celebrated as Reverend Cairncross invited them to raise their glasses in birthday greetings to 'Mark who now inherits the estates of Elrigg and to Sir Hector who now inherits the title.'

In return Mark held up his glass to Hector. 'And you, my dear cousin, have my blessing to excavate the hillfort, the standing stones and any piece of Elrigg that takes your fancy.'

Hector was delighted, and another toast was drunk to his success.

Faro was naturally suspicious of happy endings, but tonight he listened, mellowed by good wine and content with the conversations circling about him.

Across the table, Dr Brand deplored the gypsies' annual presence while Imogen Crowe defended them.

'They're not to be trusted, miss, there's always the danger that they leave our pasture gates open – they are not too fussy about bars and latches, I can tell you.'

'They aren't used to gates, Doctor. It is not part of their way of life . . .'

Faro only half listened to the argument.

'Don't you agree with me, Mr Faro?'

Not quite sure what he was expected to agree with, Miss Crowe speedily enlightened him.

'They make their annual pilgrimage to the crowning of their king at Kirk Yetholm every year.'

'Another king,' said Faro. 'Does this entail a mortal combat like your wild cattle?'

Imogen Crowe eyed him coldly. 'Not at all – the gypsy king—'

But her explanation was cut short as Hector interrupted: 'Mr Faro is fascinated by the cattle, Mark.'

'Are you indeed?' asked Poppy since Mark and his bride had their heads close together, lost in some magic world of the newlyweds. 'Do show him, Hector. The wooden box on the desk.'

Hector brought out the yellowed parchment and laid it before Faro. 'Perhaps you'd like me to read it to you: this is their earliest recorded mention – when the Scots troops occupied us in January – see, 1645:

'What with the Soldiers and this continuing Storme, if it lye but one Month more, there will bee neither Beast nor Sheepe left in the country. Your Honour's Deere and wild Cattle I fear will all dye, do what we can: The like of this Storme hath not been known by any living in the Country. The Lord look upon us in Mercy, if it be his blessed Will.'

'Fascinating,' said Faro.

'There is another account,' said Hector, warming to his subject. 'Our neighbour, the Earl of Tankerville, celebrated his son's birthday in 1756 by ordering a great number of the cattle to be slaughtered, which, with a proportionate quantity of bread, were distributed among upwards of six hundred poor people.'

'It's certainly a wonder the animals did survive.'

'They had no predators, Hector,' said the minister.

'Only man,' put in Dr Brand. 'The worst predator of all.'

But Faro shivered, as the ghost of his recurring nightmare glared down at him from the wall opposite. The head and horns of an enraged bull.

158

Chapter 24

When Faro and Vince left the Castle some hours later, dawn was breaking and the ladies had long since retired. Only Imogen Crowe remained, in earnest and, Faro admitted disgustedly, argumentative conversation.

Although she represented the new breed of womankind of whom he was a little contemptuous and a little in awe, gallantry remained. However, his offer to see her safely down the drive was scornfully rejected.

'Good heavens, no. I wouldn't dream of it.'

Alarmed in case she had misinterpreted his offer, he said hastily, 'Vince and I will be leaving in the carriage shortly.'

'Carriage, indeed. It's no distance at all and the walk will do me good. I need the exercise and you gentlemen need your port. Yes, you too, Hector,' she said firmly.

Hector looked so put out that Faro, regarding him sharply, wondered if he was in love with Miss Crowe. A situation he found personally unimaginable, although on closer acquaintance she was pretty enough and intelligent too. But he cared little for opinionated young females with their militant views regarding women's position in society.

'If they ever get the vote, heaven help us,' he said to Hector, who still looked annoyed at Imogen's rejection of his company as he shared their carriage, silently wrapped in his own thoughts.

As they prepared to retire for what remained of the night, Vince yawned: 'What a day, Stepfather. And what a curious wedding. At least Mark is one suspect you can cross off your list.'

Faro didn't care to disillusion Vince by suggesting that the possible intrigue of the pretty widow and her stepson had been neatly explained, simply to give rise to another more sinister reason for Sir Archie's demise: the obstacle to Mark's marriage had been conveniently removed.

Faro would have given much to know the exact location of Mark Elrigg, expert archer, when his stepfather died. Murders had been committed for much less than Mark's and Harriet's urgency.

Perturbed by his stepfather's silence, Vince asked: 'What do you make of Miss Crowe?'

'Not a great deal,' said Faro shortly.

'She's quite a stunner,' was the encouraging reply.

'Indeed. I hadn't noticed,' said Faro, removing his cravat. 'And what about Olivia?'

'Livvy. What about her?'

'Aren't you being, well, a little unfaithful?'

'Who said I had to be faithful to Olivia?' Vince demanded sharply.

'I presumed—'

'You presumed wrongly, Stepfather. I have no intentions but those of the friendliest towards Olivia.' He looked out of the window at the sun rising behind the standing stones. 'At present.'

Faro was thankful for those two words when Vince went on:

'Besides it wasn't for myself I was putting forward Miss Crowe as a marriageable proposition. She is a little old for me, past thirty, I should think. I had her in mind for you.'

'You – thought – ' Faro was at a loss for words.

'Indeed I did. You were getting along famously and I noticed, and I'm sure everyone else did, what a handsome pair you made.'

'Then you and everyone else are quite wrong.'

'Come, Stepfather, you really should have a wife,' Vince

sounded suddenly sober. 'You aren't all that old – in your prime, most men would say, and Rose and Emily won't always have Grandma, they would take a young stepmother to their heart.'

'Indeed? As you took a stepfather to your heart at their age,' said Faro in bitter tones that reminded Vince of how deeply he had resented his mother marrying a policeman.

'It was only until I got to know you,' Vince said meekly.

'And may I remind you that I worked very hard at that. You were an obnoxious child.' Faro grinned suddenly. 'Amazing that you turned out so well under my guidance.'

Vince shared the laughter and then Faro said sadly: 'I'll never find another woman like your mother again. If I could, I swear I'd marry her. What I don't want is a clever opinionated wife, I want someone nice, kind, loving and homely – like my Lizzie.'

Vince smiled. 'There is someone who fits that description exactly, you know, Stepfather. And she is right under your nose every day.'

Faro frowned. 'Who could that be?'

'Our housekeeper – Mrs Brook, of course.'

Faro opened his mouth, closed it again. In a voice heavy with indignation, he said, 'I have never even considered such a thing. The whole idea is quite intolerable, Vince. I trust you are joking,' he added coldly.

'Come now, Stepfather, give it a little thought. She has all the qualifications my mother had. Homely, kind, a good cook – a damned fine cook, come to that. And she is the right age for you,' he added triumphantly.

'The right age, is she?' Faro demanded. 'Nearer fifty-five than forty. Really, Vince. I'm appalled. Quite appalled. I do need a little intellectual stimulus beyond the kitchen stove and the household accounts, you know.'

'You didn't get it from my mamma, did you? But it didn't stop you loving her and producing two daughters.'

Faro was speechless as Vince went on: 'Don't you see what I'm getting at? You've come a long way since you met my Ma. Granted she was right for you then but, alas,

161

she wouldn't be right for you now. You've gone up in the world, she would never have kept up with you. You'd have left her in the kitchen long ago,' he said sadly. 'You need a wife who could enjoy the world at your pace, share your love of books and music, your vast and ever growing knowledge.'

'The kind of relationship you have with Olivia,' said Faro, determined to have the last word on marriages.

'Perhaps. Time will tell.' Vince's expression gave nothing away, but because he was equally determined, 'Like Mark and Harriet, we hope. They seem well suited. Miss Gilchrist says they have loved each other since childhood, but the vicar's daughter was not a suitable match for Sir Archie's heir. He wanted an alliance with this rich plain girl, coal owner's only daughter. But Mark and Harriet wanted each other. As you saw, true love won the day.'

Faro, listening silently, hoped it hadn't been helped by murder.

Mysteries were by no means ended and next morning yet another was thrown into the equation. Invited to accompany Owen and Olivia back to Branxton, Miss Gilchrist was extremely keen that they should see the old battlefield of Flodden and the pretty villages of Ford and Etal.

As they met in the Castle grounds, Olivia said, 'I don't know how I will ever manage to eat luncheon. Such a breakfast. I was hoping to see Miss Kent again when we said goodbye to Lady Elrigg. I'm very curious about her.'

Asked to explain, she continued, 'I am almost certain she is the same Beatrice Kent who was at boarding school in Edinburgh at the same time as I was. Of course I didn't know her very well, she was a few years ahead of me. And it was all hushed up.'

'What was all hushed up, Livvy?' asked Vince patiently, knowing her weakness for going off on a tangent.

'Protecting the younger girls from scandal, of course.'

162

'What sort of scandal?'

Olivia regarded the two men, biting her lip. 'You know, I don't even care to discuss it.'

'Oh, come along, now that you've told us this much, we're intrigued. Don't be mean, Olivia,' said Vince as she glanced uncomfortably in Faro's direction.

'Well – I don't know.'

'Oh, don't be a goose, you can tell Stepfather anything. I do.' Vince chided her gently.

'Yes, but you're different. You're a man.'

'So I've heard,' Vince laughed. 'So is Stepfather. And he has seen and heard of most of the frailties of human nature, haven't you?'

'I'm afraid so.'

'Well, what was it? Don't tell me she cheated at exams?' said Vince.

Olivia shuddered. 'Oh no, that was quite common.'

'Games, then?'

'We all cheated at games. No. It was much worse than that.'

'I know,' said Vince triumphantly. 'She flirted with the gardener's boy and was seen kissing him behind the garden shed.'

Olivia pushed him, laughing, then, suddenly serious, 'If only it was just that.'

'Surely you can't get anything more serious in a girls' boarding school than an illicit kiss with the gardener's boy—'

'Vince, listen to me, please. It was nothing like this. I mean, nothing normal.' She stopped and then went on rapidly. 'She was expelled and the music teacher dismissed.'

'That bad,' Vince whistled. 'Pupils do fall in love with their teachers, especially in girls' schools.'

'You still don't understand. We didn't have men teachers at St Grace's.'

'Oh?'

'This was a woman teacher.' Olivia gulped and blushed.

163

'They were caught – together – in bed,' she whispered.

Faro, listening to the conversation in mild amusement, did not take in the immediate significance. Girls in schools frequently slept in the same bed and his first thought was that it was the fact of a schoolgirl sleeping with one of the teachers.

But the emphasis 'together' and Olivia's accompanying blushing discomfort removed all doubts. Although he had encountered the homosexual's forbidden world during his years with the Edinburgh City Police, he found it difficult to understand – as did many of his fellow men, Vince included – that women were capable of a deep physical relationship.

Indeed, although there was a criminal law against male homosexuals there existed no such law against lesbians, simply because Her Majesty, outraged at such a suggestion, refused to believe her sex capable of such depravity.

Faro sighed. Olivia's revelations gave an added motive for murder. Two women who loved passionately and between them the unwanted husband.

'It is also one possibility', said Vince later, 'why there were no children. Sir Archie was known as a collector of beautiful objects. Presumably he regarded his lovely wife in the same light. I wonder if he knew about Miss Kent when he married her.'

'I doubt whether he would have considered it of any significance, since most rich women have companions,' said Faro.

'Perhaps he was impotent. That would account for no children by his first marriage and the adoption of his stepson as the future heir of Elrigg,' said Vince.

How ironic, thought Faro. A castle with splendid estates, a life that to the outside world had every material blessing and yet Sir Archie had every reason to envy the poorest tenants on his estate their quivers of children, many unwanted but undoubted evidence of their boundless unrestrained fertility, while his legendary sexual prowess was a lie.

'I'd like to know a great deal more about Mark's relationship with Sir Archie. From hints dropped by Aunt Molly to Olivia, which she has now confided in me, I suspect that he may well have been ill-used by him. She didn't call it that, of course, and I doubt whether he ever spelled it out even to her. But there was certainly a curious relationship between them.'

If that was so, it was indeed a motive for murder, Faro decided gloomily.

Chapter 25

Vince was to leave for Branxton with the twins and Miss Gilchrist. The latter, enchanted to learn that Miss Crowe was an authoress, had included her in the party.

Two extra passengers plus the luggage that had accompanied the twins from Edinburgh created a difficulty for the carriage, which comfortably accommodated only four people.

Heads were shaken but the problem was not insurmountable. Vince, who was required to drive the carriage, should take the twins and Miss Gilchrist. Lady Elrigg would be delighted to put the governess cart at Mr Faro's disposal if he would be good enough to take Miss Crowe with him.

Faro concealed his emotions carefully. But his sharp look in Vince's direction asked clearly as any words: if this is yet another plot to throw us together then they are in for a disappointment. He had already decided that Hector was enamoured of Miss Crowe and she had shown no evidence that she resented his attentions. In fact, through dinner at the castle, she appeared to be encouraging him.

Faro was happy to keep such observations to himself and wished the pair good fortune since it would seem to be a very suitable match – if any man were found brave enough to take on the formidable Miss Crowe.

And so the two set off for Branxton with Faro determined to be agreeable and cautious in his conversation, risking nothing that would ignite the temper that seemed to match the lady's flaming hair.

The weather was in their favour, sunny and pleasantly warm, a day to loiter in the grandeur of hill and dale. Just clear of Elrigg village, they had to pull into the side of the road to allow a troupe of gypsy caravans passage.

'On their way to Kirk Yetholm,' said Imogen, who seemed pleased at the sight of them and greeted the leading caravan in their own language.

Faro was surprised at that and she laughed. 'The Irish tongue has its uses. Besides I was brought up among their kind in Kerry. My grandmother was one of them.'

The caravans had stopped while she was speaking. A withered old woman, her hair in long white braids, leaned across so that she was level with Imogen. Toothless she smiled, obviously demanding her hand.

Imogen gave it to her reluctantly and Faro watched that dark hand holding the white long-fingered one. The gypsy said some words and Imogen gave an anxious cry and tried to withdraw her hand.

When she succeeded the old woman shrugged and turning eyes milky pale in that dark heavily seamed face upon Faro, she held out her hand in a demanding way.

Misreading the gesture he took out a coin from his pocket and gave it to her. With an indignant cry, angrily she hurled it to the ground.

'What on earth—'

'You have insulted her,' said Imogen Crowe quietly. 'She wanted to tell you something important – something written in your hand.'

'My apologies, please give her my apologies . . .'

'Oh, she understands English quite well, they just don't care to speak it if Romany will do.'

Faro turned to the old woman. 'I am sorry, I did not mean to insult you.' And, although he also didn't believe in such nonsense as fortune-telling, he gallantly held out his hand and smiled at her.

The smile won the old woman. She shrugged and took his hand, stroking it, her eyes closed, her palms surprisingly soft and warm for one so old, he thought. The soothing hands of a healer.

But he knew when she looked up at him that healing was not what she saw. Her eyes were sad, full of tears. And he knew without any explanation or translation from Imogen that the cold feeling filling his very bones was the presence of death.

His own. The silence and the stillness of that moment seemed to last for an eternity.

'No,' said Imogen sharply, as the old woman murmured. 'No,' she repeated. Then, realizing that Faro did not understand the words, she spoke to the gypsy in her own language, very gently, pleadingly.

It was enough. The cloud that had been hiding the sun vanished, the road was again filled with the noise of rattling carts, of jingling pots and pans, the smell of horses, dogs barking and children's laughter. The shadow of death had passed by and he and Imogen Crowe continued on their way as if their journey had never been interrupted.

But Faro was conscious of Imogen Crowe watching him intently, speculatively. Catching her eye, he turned away sharply.

'What was the old woman babbling on about?' he asked lightly. 'What did she want to tell me?'

'Nothing.'

'It didn't sound like nothing. Tell me what she said, I want to know, Imogen.'

She looked startled. It was the first time he had used her given name. She shook her head.

'She said I was going to die, didn't she?'

'No. No. Just that you were in terrible danger. But I could have told you that,' she added.

Faro laughed. 'Could you indeed?'

She shrugged. 'I have the sight.'

'Have you now?' Faro asked with a lightness he was far from feeling. 'Then let me tell you, young lady, there is nothing in the least remarkable about such an observation. I am a policeman and I've been in some kind of danger practically every working day of my life and I will continue to be so until death puts an end to it.'

She looked at him sadly. 'This time it is different. This danger is from within – from where you least expect it. Oh – look, over there.' She pointed to a handsome castle on the hillside.

'That's Ford.' And obviously glad to change the subject, 'King James the Fourth spent the night before Flodden there.'

'Not, I suspect, as it looks now.'

'Well, the old tower still remains, they tell me. His room with its secret staircase leading down into Lady Heron's. They were enemies; her husband and their sons were prisoners of James. Rumour has it that she was more than hospitable to the King. She wanted to get on his good side, so she used woman's only weapon. She seduced him with her charm and he was so captivated by her that, before they made love, he removed the chain of penitence that he had sworn to wear about his body until his death. True or not, it was a fatal decision.

'We don't know what happened afterwards. Perhaps he fell in love with her and she rejected him. But when he left there was ill-will between them, a sense of betrayal – so much so that he gave orders to set her castle to the torch, a poor thanks for all her kindness. Fortunately it wasn't destroyed.'

She was silent, watching the road ahead. 'But enemies they were.' And turning to him, 'You can't really ever love your enemy, despite the Sermon on the Mount, can you?'

'Why are you telling me all this? Was this part of your gypsy woman's warning?' he asked.

She smiled. 'No, I am telling you a story, that is all.'

Suddenly he remembered her book with its revealing flyleaf and that he must return it to her. He did not feel like mentioning it at that moment and he urged on the horse. She spoke no more until they climbed the steep hill to where Miss Gilchrist's house looked down on the village of Branxton with its smoking chimneys.

To their right lay the battlefield of Flodden. Its closeness made Faro uneasy, as if the carnage of that September day lingered still, never to be obliterated by even the rains of three hundred years. Nor could the blood spilt and the weeping be healed by a million larks and their rapturous song of hope and joy.

He looked down and thought that the screaming ghosts of dead and dying must forever haunt the rafters where the first swallows swooped filling the air with their gentle excited cries. And that the pale wild flowers opening in the hedgerows must be forever crimson, blood-tainted.

As they approached the house, there were voices in the garden. Miss Gilchrist, the twins and Vince were seated under a shady tree. There was the rattle of teacups, sounds of laughter.

Imogen Crowe looked at Faro, frowning. She understood. Neither were ready to exchange this sombre past for the jollity and the light-hearted banter of the present occupants of that sunny garden.

'Come with me.' Faro led the way down the hill towards the site of the battle. 'Here ten thousand men – fathers, sons, brothers – entire families – the flower of Scottish nobility – fell, wiped out in a few hours.'

At his side she said: 'Can you take it so calmly, you a Scot?'

Faro smiled. 'I'm no more Scottish than you are. I've told you that. I'm Orcadian by birth.'

She looked at him sharply. 'Of course, that's why you're so different from the rest.'

'Am I? In what way?'

She jabbed a finger at him. 'You are Viking – pure Viking. I thought that the very first day I saw you. Put a horned helmet on him, I said, and every woman within miles would run screaming—'

'I didn't realize I was such a monster as all that,' Faro interrupted in wounded tones.

'You didn't let me finish – I hadn't said in which direction they were running,' she ended impishly with a mocking coquettish glance that left him feeling not only contrite but highly vulnerable.

Chapter 26

Their arrival in the garden was greeted warmly and their long absence commented on, but as the maid brought out refreshments the weather was changing, grey skies, like an army of vengeful ghosts, creeping over the battlefield.

Miss Gilchrist shivered and said they had better go indoors.

The house was welcoming, alive with flowers, the smells of ancient wood well waxed and polished. Everything gleamed with a lifetime's devotion to crystal, pictures and furniture.

But as Faro sat in that cosy atmosphere, his eyes strayed constantly to the window overlooking the battlefield, astonished that such peace and tranquillity could exist alongside such memories of bloody carnage. A few hours that with the death of King James and his nobles altered the course of Scotland's history for ever.

After luncheon, they played at cards and, losing as he invariably did, Faro retired somewhat aggrieved to examine the well-filled bookshelves. Laughter and teasing comments echoed from the card table and he looked at the old lady so sensitive and charming, marvelling that she had lived here alone all her life. That for her each day and night would pass untroubled by the scenes the very stones on her doorstep had witnessed and remembered.

'Lucky at cards, my dear,' she said consolingly, as she also retired from the fray. 'You know what they say.'

'I don't seem to be lucky in either,' said Faro.

But Miss Gilchrist didn't hear, her eyes on Imogen

Crowe who frowned intently over her hand and then, with a whoop of triumph, threw them down, fanned wide and called: 'Game – to me!'

'Imagine Miss Crowe being an authoress,' said Miss Gilchrist admiringly.

'Depends on what – or who – she writes about,' Faro said drily. Writers made him nervous. He did not want to find himself pilloried in her next romance. A Viking indeed.

'I am sure she will be very kind to her friends. And discreet too. Perhaps she'll marry Hector.'

'You think so?'

'Yes, of course. Everyone notices that he is quite captivated by her. And she seems to encourage him. He is a fine young man and he deserves a good wife. Mark and Poppy would be pleased too. Sir Archie treated him badly.' Pausing, she studied Imogen critically. 'And she seems such a lady – for an Irishwoman.'

That made Faro laugh out loud. It was so totally out of character with his hostess. 'Are there no Irish ladies then?'

Miss Gilchrist frowned. 'There must be, I'm sure – a few. But most of the ones I've met have been gypsies or vagrants. Not very clean. And there were occasional Irish servants at the Castle in my time. Not very clean or very honest either. Twice I had coins stolen and a brooch I was fond of.'

'Perhaps poor immigrants faced with the necessity of survival cannot afford high principles,' Faro said gently. 'Famine recognizes only the fight for survival.'

When he first came to Edinburgh as a policeman in 1849, the potato famine was at its height and every boat to Glasgow and Leith was packed with Irishmen and women and their vast families, ragged, desperate, starving. A terrible sight, his mother used to weep for them and, although the Faros had little, she gave them money and food – and clothes too when they came to her door.

'God bless you – and yours,' they'd say.

That was enough for Mrs Faro. For her, money and goods had nothing to do with it. There were only good people and bad people and the good ones were welcome to her last crust.

Other than Sergeant Danny McQuinn, the only Irishmen Faro had encountered as a policeman had bombs in their pockets and were a constant threat to Her Majesty and a menace to Edinburgh's law and order. But he felt obliged, as one who also belonged to a vanquished race, to say a word or two in defence of another nation similarly and more cruelly afflicted.

'There have been noble Irish ladies,' he said, 'like Deirdre of the Sorrows.'

'Yes, indeed. Such a sad story. And so depressing, like all their legends. Never a happy ending anywhere. Indeed, when they are honest they are so mournful.'

Faro was not to be defeated. He pressed on. 'There were saints among them too. Patrick and Columba who brought Christianity from Ireland when the rest of Britain were all heathens.'

Miss Gilchrist sniffed. She was not convinced. 'But our St George was a knight,' she said proudly. 'And he slew dragons.'

They went down to the little church at Evensong. For his own reasons Faro would have preferred to remain where he was but politeness demanded that he accompanied them.

The vicar, recognizing Miss Gilchrist had brought strangers who swelled out his tiny congregation, was eager to give a good report of his church. Proudly he welcomed the visitors from the pulpit: 'These walls sheltered the dead of both warring nations after Flodden. There are no enemies once death has ruled the line. Then men are all equal, all differences forgiven in the blood of Christ.'

When they trooped out afterwards, Faro, always a practical man, considered that frenzied burial, with a nightmare vision of what ten thousand corpses heaped together looked like to the men whose task was to bury them.

Half hoping there might be some forgotten memorial

among the scattered tombstones, he wandered around reading inscriptions, deciphering weathered stones with their skulls and crossbones, their intimations of mortality.

There were names famous on both sides of the border: Elliott, Armstrong, Scott – so many young people. Thirty to forty was the average age. And there were sad reminders. A 'relict' aged nineteen, 'beloved wife aged twenty-three' with an infant one week old.

Like his Lizzie, many had died in childbirth. Children too. Died in infancy. 'Died in an accident – Elrigg – aged eleven.'

He was still staring at the stone, aware suddenly of Vince looking over his shoulder. He whistled softly and pointed to the stone. 'I think you have found your murderer, Stepfather.'

But Faro was still unconvinced.

Miss Gilchrist's party having been invited to dine with the local doctor, the twins were returning to Edinburgh next day and they had persuaded their great-aunt, much against her will, to allow Vince to sleep that night on the very comfortable sofa in the parlour.

The arrangement pleased him. 'I like to be informal and I love this house.'

Imogen Crowe declined his somewhat reluctant invitation to share the governess cart back to Elrigg. Her excuse that Hector was coming for her later was a relief for Faro, who pleaded a necessary return to the inn before setting out on holiday with Vince.

As Faro paid his bill at the Elrigg Arms, Bowden said: 'By the way, a lad came a while ago with a message from Mr Hector Elrigg. You're to meet him at the hillfort. He said it was urgent.'

The fickle weather had changed once again and it would be dark soon. A dull evening, heavy with mist, and Faro was suddenly reluctant to leave the warm fire.

Vince would say: 'Let well alone, leave it. The case is closed.'

But Faro was tempted. This might be the last link in the evidence. He told himself of course it wasn't necessary but to ferret out the truth was the habit of a lifetime. He had to know the murderer's identity for his own satisfaction, otherwise he would always be plagued by a case unfinished, a question forever poised.

He realized that the mist was thicker than ever on the road. The ground underfoot was wet with visibility limited to a few yards, a few ghostly hedgerows. He shivered as the atmosphere gripped him like a clammy shroud. Peering into the gloom, he realized that the standing stones had also vanished, hidden behind that dense grey curtain.

At the boundary fence he hesitated, caring little for the idea of crossing the open pastureland to the hillfort. The mist now clung heavily to his eyelashes, blinding him. He blinked, feeling sick with apprehension, searching the mist for shadows and finding them. He remembered being told that the cattle come down from the hill in bad weather, nearer the road, seeking shelter. Now he fancied he could hear them, the grass rustling. And smell them too.

Something rose in front of him, large and white . . .

He stood still, heart-thumping, prepared for flight as a solitary sheep rushed off bleating at his approach.

He breathed again. Then the sound of hoofs, heavy this time. A stray horse riderless swerved from his path, whinnied and disappeared.

Another shadow.

A man. The outline of head and shoulders, a soft-moving, gliding shadow.

'Hector! Hector?' he called. 'Over here.'

The air behind him was cut by a whirring sound. Instinctively, swiftly, he ducked and the arrow that was to have killed him struck his shoulder. He felt the searing agony as he staggered and tried to reach the shaft of the arrow, to drag it out, aware that he was the target for an excellent archer, one who could take his time killing him.

Through his own folly, he was going to die.

He should have listened to Vince, heeded more carefully the clues that had come his way, that pointed undeniably to the killer . . .

He heard the next arrow's flight and dropped to the ground. Through the pain, he began coughing. He felt the warm blood flowing and as the blackness of merciful unconsciousness enveloped him he fainted away.

The blackness was invaded by light, sound and smell.

He opened his eyes. At least he wasn't dead, pain told him that he was still alive. He lifted his head. It was an animal noise that had stirred him, the pounding of hoofs reverberating on the ground near him.

And then he saw it. Running towards him, the heavy head, the shining horns. For one second only, he thought he dreamed again, that this was yet another return to childhood's nightmare. But this was no shaggy red Highland beast. The animal that bore down on him with its acrid stench was the terrible reality of a white king bull.

He could not rise, in the grip of that same paralysis of nightmare. He was transfixed by fear, fear greater than the searing agony in his shoulder.

If only he could leap up . . . run . . . run . . .

And then clearly across the years he heard the voice of his aunt from that Deeside croft.

'Never run, lad. Never do that. The only way you can save yourself is to lie as still as you can. Play dead. Don't even breathe. He'll sniff at you and, if you don't move, he'll give up and go away.'

Nightmare had blocked that memory, had turned it into screaming horror. Now in the face of death again, the words had returned razor sharp, undimmed by the passing years. Knowing this was his only hope of survival, he almost lost consciousness again in those heart-stopping moments when the beast's hoofs trampled the ground inches away from his face.

He felt its hot, stinking breath on his neck, drips of saliva on his hair. Its nose touched the arrow shaft, questing, and he bit his lip hard against the scream of agony.

The smell of blood. Was that what it sought before lowering its horns into his back, lifting him bodily from the ground . . .

Every second seemed like an eternity as he waited for that terrible death.

O God – God help me . . .

And like a miracle, his prayer was answered. By a single gunshot. A second . . .

The animal grunted, lifted its nose from its quest over his body. Then he heard the hoofs beating on the ground. Growing distant.

Then no more.

No more.

Chapter 27

When he opened his eyes, it was to pain. He screamed against it but was glad even to feel pain. He was still alive.

Turning his head cautiously, he looked into the face of Imogen Crowe who held the arrow she had dragged out of his shoulder.

'I didn't know you could handle a gun.'

'Oh yes,' she smiled sarcastically. 'I use one all the time. We're never without them where I come from in Ireland. But surely you as a policeman know that.'

She lifted her head. 'Here they are. Hector's brought Dr Brand. He'll soon have you mended.' She pointed towards the fence. 'I don't know about Sergeant Yarrow. He's lying over there. In a bad way, I'm afraid.'

The two men were supported into Hector's cottage and much later, after a lot of blood and bandages, the doctor smiled at Faro.

'You're a brave man and you'll live. That shoulder will be sore for a while, but the arrow just skimmed the muscle, went sideways. You were lucky.' He looked towards the bedroom. 'Luckier than poor Yarrow.'

'Is he—'

Dr Brand shook his head. 'Not yet. But it won't be long. Took a haemorrhage from the lungs. Wouldn't listen to advice. Are you able to stand?'

'Of course.' Faro tried to swing his legs off the sofa, failed and decided against another attempt.

Dr Brand smiled. 'I couldn't help noticing as I was patching you up that you have many scars, you must have lived a very dangerous life for an insurance assessor.'

'It has its problems.'

Dr Brand nodded towards the bedroom. 'Sergeant Yarrow would like to see you.'

Faro nodded. 'Where's Miss Crowe?'

'She's in the garden. With Hector.'

'I owe her my life, you know. She scared that damned bull away.'

'You're wrong on two accounts, lad. It was Hector fired the gun. And it wasn't the king bull or you wouldn't be telling the tale. It was a cow. Maybe a young heifer.'

'A cow?'

'Yes, but her horns are just as sharp, and she can be just as dangerous. Fortunately, like all females, she suffers from curiosity. Her mate might not have wasted so much time sniffing around you.'

Faro shuddered. 'I must thank Hector.'

Dr Brand shook his head. 'Not now. See the Sergeant first. There may not be much time before Dewar gets here.'

Faro went into the bedroom quietly. At first he thought he was too late, that Yarrow was dead.

There was so little life in the face, so little difference from the colour of the pillow on which he lay, that Faro was almost taken by surprise when his lips moved: 'I should have killed you.'

'Another murder? Harder to explain away than Sir Archie.'

'How did you know?'

'I didn't. Not until I saw Eric's portrait. He was the image of you. Your eyes looked out at me. And then there was his grave in Branxton kirkyard. But most of all were your own words, first on the scene of the crime . . .'

Yarrow laughed soundlessly. 'You begin with what is certain, what you are sure of, then you build on to it.'

'The first lesson in detection, I see you still remember

179

that,' said Faro. 'My only certainty was that the killer had to be the first on the scene. And after I'd ruled out the Prince of Wales, I was left with only one man it could be – yourself.'

Faro turned round painfully and touched the sleeve of Yarrow's uniform jacket hanging over a chair. 'See, there's a button missing.'

'I know. I must have lost it.'

'And I found it. Clutched in Duffy's hand when I pulled him out of the water. The final piece of evidence, of course, was your name on the gravestone in Branxton.'

'And enough to hang me,' said Yarrow slowly.

Faro looked at him. 'Was it revenge? An eye for an eye, a tooth for a tooth?'

'Not only for my lad's death, shot by that drunken devil, but for my wife and the end of my marriage. Eric's death killed her as surely as if the bullet had struck her heart.'

He sighed, staring out of the window. 'She was never strong after he was born and he was her whole life. After he died I watched her creep steadily away from me month by month, then week by week, then each day, each hour.'

Breathless again, he paused. 'I wanted to die too when I was shot up in the Covent Garden massacre. I was pretty smashed up and they didn't expect me to survive. I was a long time in limbo, at the gates of death and to be honest I was very disappointed when they told me I would live.

'But I knew my career, my glorious future they had talked about was over. I'd never be fast on my feet again. I hated London after that and when I got the chance to come to Elrigg, it seemed that fate had taken a hand. I'm not a superstitious man, I don't believe in ghosts, but Eric started to haunt me. I dreamed of him constantly – I was obsessed, convinced that he wanted me to avenge him.

'As for Sir Archie, I was sure he'd see it on my face whenever we met – arrogant bastard that he was and me so servile: yes, sir, no, sir! But there were never any opportunities of getting him alone. I've waited years, sometimes I was with him alone but, without using my bare fists, I couldn't kill him.

180

'The first real opportunity came when we were riding escort to the Prince of Wales. We saw them disappear towards the copse and then the Prince left alone. You know the rest, Dewar set off for the village and I went to – help – Elrigg. He was unconscious and I knew I'd never get such a chance again. But what to use for a weapon? And then I remembered that the day before I'd found Bowden's bull's horns in a ditch and shoved them in my saddle bag. Evidence to nail Duffy, I thought.'

He smiled wanly. 'Now it seemed like fate, for I held in my hands a weapon to avenge my lad and make it look like an accident. I broke one of the horns off, didn't even check to see that he was still breathing in case he opened his eyes – just thrust it – hard – with both hands – into his back. It went in easily, like a stiletto. I don't know where I found the strength but he had a soft fatty body,' he added in a tone of disgust.

'I thought he groaned, but even if he wasn't dead then he had never seen my face. I hid the horn in the stone wall—'

'Where I found it.'

Yarrow smiled wearily. 'I might have guessed. And that it wouldn't take long for you to guess the rest. I hadn't bargained on Duffy either. He'd been lurking around and knew there was never a bull in sight.'

'Blackmail.'

'Yes. I paid him a few pounds but it wasn't enough and then he said he'd tell you – the insurance mannie – what he knew. I overheard him asking for you, leaving messages with Bowden and knew I had to do something about it – quick. So I arranged to meet him, promising him more money for his silence. Had a bottle with me – whisky this time. As we talked he was already drunk – and very abusive when he realized I didn't have a hundred pounds on me.

'He hit me. We both fell and struggled on the ground. I pushed his face down into the water – held him till he was dead. Then I poured the rest of the whisky over him.'

'What about Miss Halliday?'

Feebly he held up his hands. 'Not guilty. I never attacked her. I liked the woman, respected her. I'd called to collect the quarantine papers. I'd never been inside her house before. She gave me some tea, and as I sat there I saw Eric's face smiling at me.'

And Faro remembered that the abandoned cup of tea and Eric's likeness to Yarrow had helped him guess the killer's identity.

'That painting, dear God, like he was trying to speak to me. Such a likeness, tears came into my eyes. I had to have it. So I went back late that night intending to steal it. I was clumsy in my eagerness, knocked an ornament down in the dark. It smashed, she heard the noise, came downstairs, tripped and fell headlong. She never moved. I thought she was dead, took Eric's picture and ran.'

He shook his head, pale and exhausted, his voice growing fainter. 'I wasn't sure how much you knew or guessed – I didn't want to kill you – I don't suppose I'm the first.'

'By no means, Sergeant. But they were usually criminals, not honest policeman.'

'Honest,' Yarrow repeated mockingly. 'I was tired of being honest. It had got me nowhere and now I was a goner anyway. Dr Brand told me my time was up, that I could go any day. It would have been something, some small compensation to have written on my tombstone: "Here lies the man who murdered Inspector Faro of the Edinburgh City Police." Quite an epitaph. After all those famous criminals, he'd been bested by a lowly Sergeant in a country police station.'

He shook his head. 'At least there won't be enough of me to hang,' he added, indicating the silver button.

Faro handed it to him. 'Get Mrs Dewar to sew it on again.'

Yarrow looked at him in wonder. 'You mean—'

'I mean that I am going to assist a miscarriage of justice. Life has dealt you enough blows, Yarrow, blows that you are paying for dearly. You had a splendid career, an unsullied reputation. And that's how it will be remembered as far as I'm concerned.'

182

There was a message from Vince at the Inn. 'Returning to Edinburgh immediately. Had a telegraph that Balfour is in hospital. Sorry about the holiday. In haste.'

Yarrow died that night, mourned by all who knew him, especially by the Dewars who spread the word that while practising for the archery contest he had mistaken a moving shadow for one of the wild cattle looming out of the mist towards him. The arrow misfired and hit Faro a glancing blow. A sick man, the effort of pulling back the bow had caused a fatal haemorrhage.

Only Imogen Crowe and Hector Elrigg knew the truth and if Dr Brand had his suspicions then he kept them to himself.

As for Faro it seemed an unlikely explanation that might have satisfied Dewar but would have opened up an immediate inquiry for any detective inspector. The insurance mannie was a different matter.

Dr Brand signed the death certificate and the Sergeant was laid to rest. The Metropolitan Police he had served so gallantly in London most of his life as a police officer sent a representative to the funeral at Elrigg kirkyard.

No connection was ever hinted at concerning Eric Yarrow's grave in Branxton. At least, Faro thought, father and son lay only a few miles apart, to rest for all eternity under the same windswept skies, the same bird-haunted hills.

Imogen Crowe did not attend Yarrow's funeral. When they met, Faro expected that she would be announcing her engagement to Hector Elrigg.

She laughed. 'You are quite wrong, for once your deductions have played you false, Inspector Faro.'

'You would be surprised how often you are right about that,' he said bitterly.

'Just be glad you are alive – that we were in the vicinity when you fell into Yarrow's trap, his lure to get you there. You want to know why I was there that night. Hector has been courting me each time I have come to Elrigg. Perhaps this past weekend I was tempted for a while and then . . . well,' she looked at him and quickly looked away again as they eyes met.

'I intended telling him that I couldn't marry him as we drove back from Branxton. By the time we reached the hillfort the mist had got worse and I went into the cottage with him. One thing led to another, I insisted on leaving – and I wanted to walk – alone.'

She paused, embarrassed. 'Hector said if I insisted on walking back across the pastureland in heavy mist, he'd better get his gun. He carried it as a matter of course in heavy mist, when the cattle come down from the hill. A shot is all they need to scare them off. As I waited for him, I heard you calling. The mist lifted for just a moment, like a swirling shroud, and I saw Yarrow, creeping along by the fence. He was heading in your direction, loading a crossbow.'

They were both silent and then Imogen said: 'When are you leaving?'

'Tomorrow, I'm going back to Edinburgh. I wouldn't be much use on a vigorous hill-walking holiday with my arm in a sling. What about you?'

'I'm going to Ford Castle for a little while, to continue my book. I'm leaving this afternoon.'

'So am I. By train. May I offer you a lift this time?'

She smiled, remembering. 'That would be most kind. But I insist on seeing you to the station.' When he began to protest, 'I have to go into Berwick anyway. I need some more writing materials.'

On that journey they spoke little to each other.

'Will you be returning to Elrigg?' he asked.

She shook her head. 'I think not.'

There was another silence. Handing her *The History of Civilization*, he said gently, 'Your book. Tell me about Philip Gray.'

Turning, she smiled. 'What do you want to know?'

'Was he your lover?'

184

'You make that sound uncommonly like an accusation, Inspector Faro,' she said mockingly.

'None of my business,' he shrugged, trying to sound casual but sure she lied, as he saw again the words on the flyleaf. 'To my dearest Imo, with my love always, Philip G.'

'As a matter of fact,' she said slowly, 'I did love him. He was my cousin.'

'Your cousin?'

'Yes. His name was Phelan Crowe. Uncle Brendan brought us up. I went to gaol for him,' she said bitterly. 'And friends urged Phelan to change his name because of the association, so when he came to London, he became Philip Gray.'

'Was the fact that he died here what brought you to Elrigg in the first place?'

'Yes. He was more brother than cousin, you know. I had an idea someone killed him. I was like Yarrow. I wanted vengeance but I had no idea how to go about it.'

She was silent, her face sorrowful. 'I'm glad I was wrong but that Royal Family of yours has a lot to answer for.'

They reached the station as Faro's train steamed into the platform.

'Well – goodbye,' he said, taking her hand.

She brightened suddenly. 'Maybe you will have time to see me when I come to Edinburgh again.'

'Of course. Wait – I'll give you my address.'

'You'll miss your train. I can find you. I'm familiar with police stations, you know.'

The carriage door closed. The guard blew his whistle.

And Faro realized he had a great deal more to say.

As she stood on the platform and raised a hand in farewell, the sun gleamed on her hair lighting her with sudden radiance. With a whoop that was part joy of discovery, part despair he realized he had not even kissed her yet.

He had a sudden desire to throw open the door, leap back down the platform. And take her in his arms.

He saw her smile, her lips formed the words.

'Till Edinburgh!'